A BAD WEEK IN HOLLISTER

A Sheriff "Cowboy" Berkson
Mystery Novel II

Susan L. Pare'

A BAD WEEK IN HOLLISTER - All contents copyright © 2015 Susan L. Pare. All rights reserved. Printed in the United States of America.
First Edition November, 2015
All rights reserved.

Cover designed by Susan L. Pare'
ISBN-13: 978-0-9966195-2-3

Table of Contents

MORE BOOKS BY THIS AUTHOR

Red

The House on Ludington Street

What's Behind the Screen Door?

The Mayor's Son

Willerton Woods

Cowtown

Floating Face Down
A Sheriff "Cowboy" Berkson Mystery Novel – Book Three

Let's Play Autopsy

A Bad Week In Hollister
A Sheriff "Cowboy" Berkson Mystery Novel – Book Two

Don't Smother Your Mother
A Sheriff "Cowboy" Berkson Mystery Novel – Book One

Crossing Sydney

Blueberries and Bears and My Brother's Shoes
First Edition – out of print

"You remember him. He lost his wife a couple of years ago when one of those Ride the Ducks boat thingies ran over her."

"Yeah. I remember him. That was one freaky accident. She never saw it coming."

"She was blind, Casey. Of course, she never saw it coming."

Dedication

Thank you to my wonderful family and friends, who buy my books and read them.

To all my fans that leave those great reviews – thank you for your support.

To Wendy VanKlei - thanks for continuing to proof my books. Finding those missing "quote" marks is a job unto itself.

To all the people who voted on the book cover. Thanks for your input, which only made the choice harder.

I'm so grateful to be able to do this, especially at this point in my life. So, the biggest thank you is to God, who gave me my writing talent, such as it is.

A BAD WEEK IN HOLLISTER

A Sheriff "Cowboy" Berkson
Mystery Novel II

Sylvia Toppers

She fought hard. She knew she was fighting for her life, but Sylvia couldn't remove the hand that was holding her head under water. She finally gave in to her body's demand for air and took a deep breath. She sucked in pool water, and it went deep into her lungs. It didn't take much more before everything went dark, and she gave in to the peaceful feeling that enveloped her. There was no last thought, as her mind had already stopped functioning.

Suddenly, she felt a slap on her cheek. "Sylvia, wake up. Come on, girl." Another slap. She coughed hard, turned on her side, and expelled some of the water that had filled her lungs.

"That's it. I was afraid you had died on me."

He watched as she coughed a few more times. Finally, he picked her up and carried her into his house. "Can you walk, Sweetheart?"

Sylvia shook her head. She coughed again and brought up more water from her lungs.

"No? Well, you just rest a few minutes and I'll get you out of those wet clothes. How does that sound?"

He laid her on his bed and slowly undressed her, his fingers caressing her breasts, as he removed her blouse and bra. "Does that feel good? You have beautiful breasts, you know."

As he removed the remainder of her wet clothes, Sylvia stayed quiet. He helped her sit up and put a soft terry cloth robe on her, covering her nakedness.

"I wonder how many men have told you that. How many men had cupped your breasts in their hands and sucked on those nipples? Can you even remember them all?"

He gently stroked her face, smiling down at her.

"I want you to rest now. You're in for a long night," he said and left the room.

The room was dark when Sylvia woke up. She heard voices coming from the living room and wondered who else was in the house. After she heard music playing, she realized the noise was coming from a TV. She stood up, her legs a little shaky, and tried to open the bedroom door. It was locked.

She sat on the edge of the bed, trying to decide her next move. She glanced over at the window, wondering if she could make it to the woods. If he had the alarm on, she didn't have a chance. She knew the odds were against her. She also knew he was probably going to kill her. She walked over to the window, unlocked it, and opened it. Immediately, the alarm sounded, startling her. She started to crawl out the open window, but he grabbed her ankles and pulled her back into the room.

"Seriously, Sylvia? I thought you were smarter than that. Get up."

Sylvia stood up and faced him. "Enough. Please, just let me go home."

"Not until you tell me."

"I can't tell you something I don't know. I told you I don't know."

"Tell me," he yelled. "I'm not messing around any longer." He grabbed her and pulled her closer, wrapping a hand around her throat. "I'll kill you where you stand."

Sylvia tried to pull his hand away, but he tightened his grip, pushing his fingers deeper into her throat. She gagged, as he slowly started to choke the life out of her. He watched her face, as unconsciousness overcame her and she became limp. He let go and she dropped to the floor.

When she finally opened her eyes, he was sitting in a chair, watching her, "You are a survivor. Did you know that, Sylvia? You've been close to death twice tonight. Yet, here you are. Still breathing. You don't look so well, though. Can you talk?"

She tried to speak, but no words came out. Her throat hurt. Sylvia shook her head no.

"What am I ever going to do with you? One more chance, Sylvia. Who killed Melissa? Was it Bobby?"

Sylvia looked up at him and smiled. Fuck you, she mouthed.

He stood up and kicked her hard in the ribs. She moaned and curled up into a ball. He kicked her again and walked out of the room.

Sylvia came to in the back seat of a moving car. Her car. She stayed quiet, staring out the window, trying to figure out where she was. It was dark, but the night was clear and she could see the stars shining brightly.

The car came to a stop and the driver got out. He opened up the door to the back seat and smiled. "Sylvia, my dear, I'm so glad you woke up. It's always more fun when you're awake. However, it's time to end this. You got yourself into this mess, you know. If I let you go, you're sure to go to the police. I can't have that. You leave me no choice."

Sylvia looked at him with pleading eyes and shook her head no.

"No, I shouldn't kill you or no, you won't go to the police?" he asked.

"Uh, uh, no police," she whispered.

"I wonder why I don't believe you," the man said, as he raised the gun he held in his hand and shot her.

He pulled her out of the car onto the ground. He took the soft terry cloth robe off her dead body and placed it into a large plastic bag. Then, he dragged her dead body down the small incline to the lake, and pushed her into the water.

"I shall miss you, my love," he said.

Twenty minutes later, he pulled over to the side of the road and stopped. He turned off the car, wiped down the steering wheel with a cloth, and got out. He walked to the back of the car and removed his bike from the trunk. Using the cloth once more, he wiped off the areas where he had touched the trunk and the door handles. He got on his bike and rode off. It was still dark, it was very late, and he was sure no one saw him.

"She's dead," the man said.

What do you mean, she's dead? You weren't supposed to kill her."

"It got a little out of hand. I gave her plenty of chances, but she wouldn't talk."

"Where is she?"

"She's fish food," he said and ended the call.

Sunday Morning

Deputy Casey George came charging through the door to find Sheriff Jason 'Cowboy' Berkson sitting at his desk, feet up, reading the Hollister Newsletter.

"Just ran into Sam Fillerman," he said, out of breath and puffing hard. "He told me Myrtle claims she saw a body floating in the lake."

"Calm down, boy. You're about to keel over. You talking about Myrtle down at the bait shop?"

"Yes, sir."

"Why is she telling Sam and not me? I haven't had no phone calls about a floater."

"Don't know, Sheriff," the deputy answered. "I figure we should check it out, though."

"Guess so," said the sheriff. "Grab Funtelli and get over there. Let's see what all the noise is about."

"Just gotta take a leak and I'll get right on it," Casey said and headed for the head.

Deputy George stood on the shoreline, talking on his cell phone to the sheriff while looking down at a body,

"We got a dead one, all right," Casey told the sheriff. "You'll never guess who it is."

Who?" asked the sheriff.

"Take a guess."

"This is not a guessing game, Casey," Sheriff Berkson yelled. "Just tell me who the hell it is."

"You're never gonna believe it, Sheriff. It's Sylvia Toppers."

"Seriously? The woman who lives out on Harper Road?"

"Yep. The same one. It doesn't look to me that she's been in the water very long," Casey told him.

"Have you called Doc? You need to get the coroner out there right now."

"Funtelli just called him. He'll be here in a few minutes," Casey said.

"I'm coming over. Don't touch anything. Who took her out of the lake?"

"Myrtle. She said she couldn't stand seeing her bobbing up and down out there, so she jumped in her boat and went and got her. When she reached her, she tied a rope around one of her legs and pulled her through the water to shore. Then, she dragged her out of the water with the rope she had tied to her leg.

"Good god," said the sheriff. "Well, so much for ruining evidence, if there was any."

"That's not all," said Casey.

"What else," the sheriff sighed.

"She covered her up with an old tarp, full of fish scales and crap. She didn't want anyone to see a naked body."

"How does she look?" asked the sheriff.

"I only moved the tarp enough to get a look at her face, sheriff. But, with the hole in her forehead, I'd make a pretty good guess that this was no accident."

"Shit," said the sheriff. "Stay put. I'm on my way."

Shortly after he arrived, Doc Harris, the Coroner of Taneycomo County, declared Sylvia Toppers dead. He told Sheriff Berkson and his deputy that he was pretty sure she died from a gunshot to her head.

"I'm still going to have to perform an autopsy to determine the cause of death," Doc Harris told the sheriff.

"So, you figured she was shot before she was tossed in the water, Doc?" the sheriff asked him.

"Doesn't make much sense to drown her first and then shoot her, does it?" replied the Coroner.

"No, I guess not," said the sheriff.

"It seems you have a real crime spree going on here, Cowboy. First, Melissa Johnson's son smothers her, and now Sylvia Toppers is shot. Weren't they neighbors?" Doc Harris asked.

"They lived down the road from each other, up there on Harper Road. You remember her, don't you, Doc? Sylvia testified against John Johnson at his trial. I guess you could say she put him in jail for life."

"That's right. Well, it looks like you have your hands full and I have work to do. Good luck figuring this one out, Cowboy."

"Let me know what you find, Doc," the sheriff said.

"Always do," answered Doc Harris, as he walked away.

"So, what do you think, Sheriff?" Casey asked him. "Do you think Melissa being killed and now this, with Sylvia, could be connected? It sure seems more than a coincidence to me."

"Don't jump the gun here, Casey. Let's go where the evidence leads us," said the sheriff.

"What evidence?" Casey asked. "I sure as hell don't see any evidence."

"It's someplace. There's always evidence. We just have to find it," said the sheriff.

"Start here and work backwards, right?" Casey asked.

"You got it, Casey. Let's start canvassing the area. Maybe somebody saw something. Start with Myrtle."

"I already talked to her," Casey told him.

"Well, talk to her again. Maybe she remembers something else."

"Sheriff, have you ever talked to her? It's like having a conversation with a fish."

"She has her good moments. You just never know with her. Where's Funtelli? Get him over here," the sheriff said.

Deputy George looked around and saw Officer Simon Funtelli talking to a couple of men he did not recognize. He waved at Funtelli and motioned to him to come over. Officer Funtelli waved back, said something to the men, and walked over to Casey.

"Sheriff wants you," said Casey.

"What's up, Sheriff?" asked Officer Funtelli.

"I want you to go question Myrtle. See if she remembers anything else. Then, I want you to come down here every day and question her again."

"Every day?" the officer asked.

"Every single day until this case is closed. You just never know what might pop into that brain of hers," said the sheriff.

"What the hell you punishing me for, Sheriff?" Officer Funtelli whined. "What did I do?"

"Hell, Funtelli. You didn't do anything. It's just that you're so damned cute, women can't stand it," the sheriff said, laughing.

"But, Myrtle, Sheriff? She doesn't even know what day it is. There's little chance that by tomorrow she'll even remember pulling that body out of the water."

"If anyone can get her to remember, it'll be you. Now get your ass over there and see what she has to say," the sheriff told him.

Sunday Afternoon

Except for a coffee cup sitting in the sink, Sylvia Topper's house was immaculate. There were no signs that any struggle or murder had taken place in any room of the house. Sheriff Berkson was going through her desk, looking at old bills and bank records.

"It doesn't look like she was in debt. Her house and car are free and clear and she paid her credit card charges in full every month. I remember her telling me that she got alimony from her ex and that she did some kind of work on the computer. 'Enough to get by,' is what she told me," the sheriff said to his deputy.

"Doesn't she have a sister down in Texas?" Casey asked him.

"Good memory there, Casey. Yep, down in Corpus Christi. We need to get her name and give her a call. Let her know about Sylvia. See if you can find something around here with her name on it and. . . . Well, this is interesting."

"Whatcha got there, Sheriff?"

"Will you look at this? Looks like she did a lot more than just get by. This here statement shows she has almost a million dollars sitting in an account in Springfield."

"Maybe she did better in her divorce settlement than she let on," Casey commented.

"Don't think so," replied the sheriff. "This money was deposited around a year ago."

"That's just about the same time Big John was sent to prison," Casey said. "I'm telling you, Sheriff, I've got a bad feeling about this."

"We need Brad to go through her computer and phone. Pack it all up and we'll take it back to the office."

"Think he'll find anything?" asked Casey.

"No idea, but we need to take a look," replied the sheriff.

Two hours later the sheriff and his deputy were back at the police station, discussing their next move. They had turned the electronics from Sylvia's house over to Officer Brad Herzberg, the resident computer expert, for examination.

"Think Brad will find anything?" Casey asked the sheriff.

"I didn't know the last time you asked me, and I don't know now," the sheriff replied.

"Right," said Casey. "Have you heard from Doc Harris yet?"

"It's a little soon, although we should get a prelim from him sometime yet today."

"What do you think killed her?" asked Casey.

"Well, for starters, I figure the shot to her forehead had something to do with it. What the hell is wrong with you? You saw the body. What do you think killed her?" the sheriff asked him.

"Sorry, Sheriff. I didn't get much sleep last night."

"That baby still not sleeping all night?" asked the sheriff.

"Up every three hours. She's driving me nuts."

"It'll get better," the sheriff told him.

"God, I hope so."

"I think I'm gonna take a drive. Want to ride along?" the sheriff asked him. "Maybe a little fresh air will help clear your head."

"Can we stop for a cup of fresh coffee?" the deputy asked him.

"Sure thing."

"Where are you going?" Casey asked.

"Thought I'd see if Bobby Johnson is home."

Bobby Johnson was Melissa Johnson's only son who was not sitting in jail. His youngest brother, Tom, was serving a fifteen-year sentence for attempting to kill their mother. Big John, his oldest brother had been convicted a few weeks later, of actually killing her, and would be spending the rest of his life in jail.

Before Bobby's mother was murdered, she had inherited millions of dollars when her father died. Now, Bobby was sitting pretty, being the sole beneficiary of her estate.

Bobby was a good-looking man, loved to eat and drink and, due to his excesses, tended to be a little on the heavy side. He hated to exercise but found that if he swam for an hour or so a day, he could keep the excess weight off and stay trim. He had a heated, Olympic-sized pool in his backyard and, unless he was out of town, never missed a day getting his daily exercise.

The sheriff and his deputy sat in the squad car, staring at Bobby's property.

"How much do you think all this cost?" Casey asked the sheriff.

"A small fortune. Which he has. You have to admit that it's beautiful. You just don't see grass like that around here. Look at that shed. It's huge."

"He has three or four different vehicles, besides his truck. Must be nice to be so rich," said Casey.

"The house is huge. No way in hell anyone would ever call that a trailer. Looks like the woods in back have been cleared, too."

"Had to make room for his pool," Casey told him.

"His what? He has a pool back there?"

"It's totally fenced in, too. Remember all that blasting a while back? It took forever to get through all those rocks. I hear it's beautiful."

"Well," said the sheriff, "let's go take a look."

Bobby answered his door on the first knock. When he saw the sheriff and his deputy standing there, his expression immediately changed, expressing his disdain.

"Afternoon, Bobby. Mind if we come in for a few minutes?"

"What's up, Sheriff? I'm out of brothers for you to arrest."

"I'll only take a couple of minutes of your time," the sheriff said, as he walked by Bobby and into the living room. "Mind if we sit?"

"Go ahead," Bobby said, as he plopped himself into a huge recliner.

"Sylvia Toppers is dead, Bobby. It looks suspicious and I'm wondering if you saw any strange vehicles around here during the past twenty-four hours."

"Sylvia's dead? What happened? Some type of accident?"

"We're still investigating and can't say too much on the subject right now. We're just trying to put all the pieces together. You knew her, right?"

"Of course, I did. She's the reason Big John's in jail. She made a mistake there, you know. He didn't kill my mother, but she did think she saw his truck parked there that night. You know, I actually dated her a few times, but it didn't work out. She was a nice lady, but I just couldn't get past her testifying against Big John. I'm sorry to hear that she's gone."

"When's the last time you saw her?"

"Last night. She waved at me as she drove by the house."

"What time was that, Bobby?" the sheriff asked.

"I'm not entirely sure. I think it was probably around six or six-thirty."

"Where were you last night," Casey asked.

"I was at Waxy's most of the night, having a few with some friends."

"Can anyone verify that?" asked Casey.

"I would imagine quite a few could. We could start with the woman in my bed, who spent the night and has been here all day. You want to go wake her up?"

"I think we'll pass for now," the sheriff said, chuckling.

"Anything else, Sheriff?" Bobby asked.

"You're looking good, Bobby. Taking good care of yourself?" the sheriff asked him.

"I do what I can. It's lonely, though, with everyone gone."

"Hear you built yourself a big old swimming pool. Mind if we take a look?" asked the sheriff.

"Help yourself," Bobby said, stood up, walked to the door overlooking the backyard, and opened it.

The sheriff and his deputy stood in the doorway, staring at the pool.

"It's big," said the sheriff.

"Really big," said Casey.

Monday Morning

Officer Funtelli sat in his squad car, drinking a fresh cup of hot coffee. He didn't want to get out and go talk to Myrtle. Not today or tomorrow or the next day. His only hope was that the sheriff would solve this case as fast as possible, and this assignment would be over.

He sipped his coffee slowly, killing time. He watched Jake, Myrtle's husband, leave the bait store, get in his truck, and drive away. Crap, he thought, my only buffer is gone. Now I have to face Myrtle alone.

Deciding he could no longer put off the inevitable, Funtelli got out of the car and walked over to the store. Myrtle was standing at the counter with her hands in a container that held worms.

"Morning, Myrtle. I know you're busy, but I just need to ask you a few questions. It's about that woman you pulled out of the lake yesterday."

"Just look at the size of this worm," Myrtle replied, shoving the worm at Funtelli's face.

The officer took a step back. "Nice," he said. "So, tell me what you saw yesterday."

"Saw me a dead lady," replied Myrtle. "She wasn't in a boat and was swimming too far out in the water. I think she musta got hit by a boat and drowned."

"Did you see a boat out there?" the officer asked.

"She wasn't in a boat."

"I know, Myrtle. But, did you see any boats out there when you first noticed her?"

"You are very handsome," she replied.

"Thank you. Can you think about it for a minute, Myrtle? Do you remember seeing any boats out in the lake near the woman?"

"Hell, if there weren't no boats, Jake and me would be out of business. People buy our worms and stuff to go fishing in their boats. I see boats from the time I get here until I leave. Unless we have a big flood like we had that one time. You wanna buy some worms? Just look at this big fat one I found."

"Did you see any strange cars or people acting suspiciously yesterday?"

Myrtle thought for a few seconds before she answered. "I sure did," Myrtle finally told him.

"You did? Do you remember what they looked like?" Funtelli asked her.

"Well, I guess I do. I seen some black cars and some gray cars. I remember seeing a red truck. Hell, almost every car I see is strange. I seen some weird people, too. You can't believe how . . . "

"Got it," Funtelli said, interrupting her. "You deal with weird people who drive strange vehicles. Okay, Myrtle, that's it for today. I'll be back tomorrow to see if you remember anything else."

"You coming back tomorrow? How 'bout you bring us some donuts? Jake and me just love donuts."

"Donuts, it is," said Funtelli, as he headed out the door.

"Hey, handsome," Myrtle yelled, causing Funtelli to turn and look at her.

"Make sure a couple of those donuts are jelly-filled. I sure do love me jelly donuts."

Officer Funtelli smiled at her and continued to walk to his squad car. He got in the car and seriously considered taking out his service revolver and shooting himself in the head.

Doc Harris walked into the Hollister Police Station and handed the sheriff an envelope. The Doc's expression was not a happy one.

"Morning, Doc," said Sheriff Berkson. "I'm thinking you being here means bad news."

"Morning," replied the Doc.

"Autopsy report?"

"My prelim. Blood test will be back this afternoon or tomorrow."

"You didn't have to drive all the way over here to give them to me. You could have just called," said the sheriff.

"I could have. But, then, I wouldn't get to see the look on your ugly face when you read my report."

"It's bad?" asked the sheriff.

"It's bad," replied Doc Harris.

Sheriff Berkson opened the envelope, took out a sheet of paper, and started reading. After a few seconds, he looked up at Doc and said, "You have got to be shitting me."

"Never expected that, did you?" Doc asked him. "There's more."

The sheriff finished reading the rest of the report, put it on his desk, got up, and walked over to the coffee machine. "You want a cup?" he asked Doc Harris.

"No, thanks."

Sheriff Berkson sat down, leaned back, and put his feet up on his desk. He stared at Doc for a few seconds, not exactly sure how to put his next question.

"So, she was kind of drowned, choked, but not to death, shot in the head, and then thrown in the lake? How the hell are you kind of drowned?"

"That's your question?" the Doc said, laughing.

"That's my first question," the sheriff replied.

"She had a lot of water in her lungs like she had been held under for a while. But that didn't kill her."

"Well, what did?"

"The obvious killed her, which is being shot in the head. However, she was choked before she was shot. There are bruises on her neck and her hyoid bone was bruised, but not broken, which indicates some type of strangulation."

"How can you tell what came first? I mean, how do you know she almost drowned before she was choked?"

"The way I figure it," the Doc replied, "is that if she had been choked first, the damage to her hyoid bone wouldn't have allowed her to expel enough of the water to keep her from drowning. It's very complicated."

"No shit, Doc. So, you're telling me that all this took place on a boat. It would have had to, right, if it went down like you said. Almost drowning, choking, shooting, and then dumping her in the lake."

"Not exactly."

"There's more?" the sheriff asked.

"A test we ran showed that the water in her lungs wasn't lake water."

"Don't tell me. It had chlorine in it."

"Yep. Sure did."

"Pool water. Son of a biscuit. Bobby Johnson has a pool. Casey had this one figured out all the time."

"You have any other evidence against him, Sheriff? Because there are a whole bunch of swimming pools around here. You may have to start checking every one of them before you find the right one," Doc said.

"Plus, Bobby has an alibi," the sheriff said.

Michael McMillan

Michael McMillan's home sat high on a cliff, overlooking Lake Taneycomo. It was big, beautiful, and private. A professional landscaper cared for the yard, and a pool service came twice a week to maintain the large kidney-shaped pool.

Steps were leading to the lake but rarely used, as the climb was extremely steep and dangerous. After a friend had taken a serious fall, Michael had spent a small fortune to have a lift installed for easy, safe access to his boathouse and dock.

Michael was thirty-nine years old, shamefully handsome, and divorcing his third wife. He loved women. He just didn't like being married, which he conveniently forgot until he was married again.

After his third wife, Candy, moved out, Michael decided to limit his dating to just a few women. He wasn't looking for a serious relationship or a new wife. At this point, all he wanted was an occasional dinner date, with a little sex thrown in.

Sylvia Toppers was one of those women who fit his requirements. She was extremely good-looking and fun to be around. On their third date, she casually mentioned that, just like him, she wasn't looking for a serious relationship either.

That was probably the worst thing she could have told him. Michael always wanted what he couldn't have, and he decided, at that moment, that she would be his next wife.

Michael was a sharp businessman. He knew how to negotiate a deal to get what he wanted and he used the same tactics with Sylvia. He started slow, suggesting a trip to Vegas. She thanked him but said no. He was shocked at the refusal.

A week later, when they were out for dinner, he asked her to fly to Paris with him. He had a business meeting, he told her, and thought she might enjoy the sights and shopping. She said she would have to think about it. The next day, he called and pressured her for an answer. She told him it wasn't convenient for her at this time. He couldn't figure out what he was doing wrong, so he backed off to consider his next move. She was becoming more of a challenge than he cared to admit.

A week later, Sylvia agreed to have lunch with him at his home. They spent a wonderful afternoon talking, swimming in his pool, and making love. When she started to leave, he asked her to wait; he had something to ask her first, and he left the room.

Sylvia was sitting on his couch, looking out at the beautiful view, when Michael walked into the room, smiling. He stood in front of her for a few seconds, looking down at her. Then he dropped to one knee, held out a diamond ring, and asked her to marry him.

Sylvia looked at him as if he was a spot on the rug that wouldn't come out while wondering if there was any cleaner on the market that would work. Then, unfortunately, instead of politely refusing him, she laughed.

"This is all a joke, right?" she asked, with a slight giggle.

"I take it that's a no," replied Michael.

Sylvia stood up. Michael pushed her back down into the chair. "You're laughing at me. I want to marry you, and you think this is all a joke?"

"Michael, settle down. I don't want to marry you or anyone. I told you I didn't want to get serious. I don't love you. I'm sorry, but I just don't. I need to leave now."

"I don't understand," Michael said. "I thought we were having fun."

"We are. But that doesn't mean we have to get married. I like you. I'd like to stay friends. You just have to back off a little. My god, Michael, you're not even divorced yet and you want to get married again. You seriously have to learn to slow down and think about what you're doing."

Michael was now sitting on the floor, looking up at her. She could see the anger slowly leave and regret step in.

"I'm sorry, Sylvia. I want to be friends. I hope I haven't destroyed that. Forgive me."

"Of course, I forgive you. Actually, I'm flattered. I just don't want to get married again."

Michael stood up, took her hand, and helped her out of the chair. "Still friends?" he asked.

"Of course. Now, I do have to leave."

Michael watched Sylvia walk to the door, open it, and leave.

"Turn me down, will you, bitch," he muttered to himself. "You just made the biggest mistake of your life."

Monday Morning - Two

"How many pools do you figure there are in Hollister?" Casey asked the sheriff.

"Probably a hundred. I figure there might be more than a thousand in Branson. There's no way we can search them all. I figure we are looking for someone who has a pool or access to one, though."

"You think the water came from a pool? Maybe it was a bathtub," Casey remarked.

"I don't think so. There was chlorine in the water in her lungs, remember? I want to get water samples from some of the pools. The levels of chlorine and PH in pool water change all the time, but Doc Harris can analyze the chemical makeup. If we got a match, we could use a filtered sump pump to try to collect some trace evidence. We might get lucky and find a hair or something," The sheriff said.

"Have you contacted Sylvia's sister down in Corpus Christi yet?"

"I did," the sheriff told him. "She's coming up to make the arrangements for her sister's funeral. We should head over and go through Sylvia's house one more time. Make sure we didn't miss anything."

"I don't think we missed anything," Casey said.

"Did you find an address book when you went through her stuff?"

"Brad said he found one in her computer. He was supposed to print it out. He's checking all the phone numbers that were in her cell, too."

Sheriff Berkson threw a pencil across the room at Brad, who was working at his desk. The pencil hit the corner of the desk, startling him. "You need something, Sheriff?" he asked.

"You got that list of names and phone numbers?" the sheriff asked him.

"It's on your desk, Sheriff."

The sheriff looked through a stack of papers until he found what he was looking for. He read it, put it down, and looked at Casey.

"We are gonna be busy," the sheriff told him.

"Why's that?"

"Because, at least eleven people on that list have swimming pools, and six of them are single men."

"How do you know they have swimming pools?" Casey asked him.

"Brad checked the list to see who had pools."

"Really? He does good work, doesn't he?" Casey commented.

"He's the best. I wonder who Sylvia might have been dating besides Bobby Johnson," the sheriff said.

"Who else on that list, besides Bobby, has a pool? I didn't know there were that many pools around here," Casey said.

"A couple of them are those round ones that sit on the grass. The rest are what they call below-ground pools. Cement ponds, I think the Clampets called them."

"Who are the Clampets? They from around here?" Casey asked him.

"You ever watch the Beverly Hillbillies, Casey?" the sheriff asked him.

"You know somebody named Beverly Hillbilly?"

"Not Beverly Hillbilly. The Beverly Hillbillies."

"They live in Hollister?" Casey asked him.

"Forget it," replied the sheriff, shaking his head in frustration.

"Who else is on the list?" Casey asked him again.

"I think we should talk to all of them. We already talked to Bobby Johnson, but I think we should talk to him again. Then there's George Adams. "

"George Adams can hardly walk. I doubt he had anything to do with Sylvia's death."

"He's up there in years, for sure, but we should still question him. We can't rule anyone out yet," said the sheriff.

"Who else?"

"Michael McMillan. He owns that big house overlooking the lake. I hear he's getting rid of wife number three. Steve Leyson lives on Deer Run Road. You remember him. He lost his wife a couple of years ago when one of those Ride the Ducks boat thingies ran over her."

"Yeah. I remember him. That was one freaky accident. She never saw it coming."

"She was blind, Casey. Of course, she never saw it coming."

"I didn't mean it that way," Casey said, laughing.

"You know a Chuck Oberson?" the sheriff asked him.

"I never heard of him. Is he on the list?" Casey replied.

"Lives on Kays Lane," the sheriff told him.

"Is that all?"

"One more we should check. Jimmy Johnson. No relation to Bobby. He's a mean one. I arrested him a couple of times for starting fights. His daddy was Lester Johnson. He owned Johnson's Feed and Grain. Jimmy came into a lot of money, after his dad died, and bought himself a big house out there past the high school. It's got a pool, too."

"We gonna start with the six men?" Casey inquired.

"Gotta start someplace."

"Any single women on that list with swimming pools?"

"You gotta wife, Casey. You don't need to be checking out single women," the sheriff said, laughing.

"I like the one I got, Sheriff. But, these days, you can't tell who is going with who. Maybe our Sylvia liked both men and women."

"That's a thought. Well, let's start checking the men first," the sheriff said while turning his chair to get Brad's attention. "Brad, did you check that list for single women who might have swimming pools?"

Brad gave him a shit-eating grin, and said, "Never even considered that it might be a woman. I'm on it, Sheriff."

"We need to pick up some pint jars for the water samples. Where's the best place to get some?"

"Lowes should have them," Casey said. "We need warrants, Sheriff?"

"Hell, no. You're gonna fill those jars with pool water, while I question them. I'll haul their asses in if they don't like it. If Doc finds something, then I'll get a warrant. No sense bothering the D.A.'s office for no reason."

"You wanna get lunch first? It's gonna be a long afternoon." Casey asked.

"Good idea. Let's walk over to Minnie's Diner."

"Sheriff, didn't Sylvia have a car?"

"Sure, she did. She drove a . . ." The sheriff stopped talking in mid-sentence and looked at his deputy. "My god, her car. Her car wasn't at her house. How the hell could you forget about her car, Casey?"

"Like I'm the only one," Casey said.

"Brad," the sheriff yelled.

"What?"

"Put out an APB on Sylvia Topper's car. Now."

Monday Afternoon

"Man, I'm stuffed," Casey told Sheriff Berkson, as they left the restaurant. "Minnie's portions are huge."

"You sure didn't have any trouble cleaning your plate," the sheriff replied. "I think we should start with George Adams. I figure one visit and we'll be able to cross him off our list."

"How old is he, anyway?" Casey asked.

"I'm not really sure. He's probably in his sixties, but it's hard to tell. He spends a lot of time out by his pool, and the sun can sure age you."

"Is his wife dead?"

"She left him twenty years ago. I don't think they ever got divorced."

The sheriff and his deputy parked in front of the Adams' house. Casey got out, opened one of the car's back doors, and removed a pint jar from a cardboard box. "You figure we should have washed these before we use 'em?" he said.

"They should be okay," the sheriff said, as he got out of the squad car. "Just check to be sure there aren't any bugs or dirt in them. You go get some of the pool water and I'll see if anyone is home."

The sheriff walked to the front door and rang the bell. Casey walked to the backyard, saw a tall fence, but no gate. Figuring that the gate was on the other side of the fence, he walked back the way he had come. As, he walked by the sheriff, who was still standing at the front door, he asked, "No answer?"

"Where you going?" the sheriff asked him.

"Looking for a gate. The yard is fenced."

The door swung open and a young woman, in her early twenties, stood there, smiling at the sheriff. "Good afternoon. What can I do for y'all?"

"Afternoon, ma'am. Is George home?"

"Y'all that sheriff they call Cowboy, ain'tcha?" she asked.

"Sure am. I just need to ask George a couple of questions. Is he here? Sorry, I didn't get your name."

"That's 'cause I didn't give it to y'all. I'm Kitty Adams. George is my grandpa. Or, rather he was. He died last night. He wasn't even sick and then he just up and died. Just like that. We sure are gonna miss him. I loved him so much," Kitty said and started to cry.

"I'm sorry for your loss. I was wondering if you have any idea where your grandpa might have been Sunday night or early this morning."

"I sure do," Kitty replied.

The sheriff waited a few seconds. The tears stopped as fast as they had started, and Kitty smiled at him.

"And – that would be?" he prompted.

"Oh, silly ol' me. You want to know. He was here with us, Sheriff. My daddy and I have been visiting him since Wednesday. Last night we cooked out, watched a little TV, and went to bed. He was here all the time."

"Thank you for your time. Again, my condolences to you and your family."

As the sheriff headed back to the car, Casey rounded the corner of the house. The sheriff started the car, turned on the AC, and waited for Casey to get settled.

"I think I'm going to be sick," Casey said, as he tried to hand the sheriff the bottle filled with pool water.

"Don't give me that crap. What the hell is in there?" the sheriff asked. "That water is green."

"From the looks of it, that pool hasn't been cleaned in years. There was a dead squirrel floating on a slimy rubber raft, right there in the middle of the pool. It's disgusting, that's what it is."

"We don't need the water, Casey," the sheriff said, laughing. "We can scratch George off the list. He's dead. He died last night."

"You mean I stuck my hand in that contaminated water for nothing? Thanks a lot, Sheriff."

"It comes with the job, my friend. Here - dump this water out. I don't need it stinking up my car."

"I need to go wash my hands," Casey said.

"We'll stop at Ken's Station and you can wash up there," the sheriff told him.

The sheriff decided they should drive over to Michael McMillan's house next. He was in the car, waiting for Casey to finish up in the gas station, when a red Ferrari drove by, headed towards town.

"Well, I guess McMillan isn't home," the sheriff said, to no one.

Casey opened the car door and handed a Big Gulp to the sheriff. "Thanks," the sheriff said, as he took the drink from Casey. "We're skipping McMillan for now."

"Why's that?" Casey asked.

"He just drove by headed to town,"

"We can still get some water, can't we?"

"You're right. Let's go get some of Mr. McMillan's pool water."

Sheriff Berkson turned off the main road and drove down the long driveway. He pulled up to the front entrance of

Michael McMillan's house and stopped the car. "I'll try the door," he said to Casey, "I doubt anyone is here, though. Go get a sample from his pool."

"I'm on it," Casey said and started to get out of the car. He immediately jumped back in and closed the door, as a huge Doberman came running at the car.

"That was close," the deputy said.

"He's not barking," the sheriff said. "He looks friendly enough. His tail's wagging. Go ahead and get the sample. I don't think he's mean."

"How about I wait while you go knock on the door?" Casey replied.

"I have a phone call I need to make first," the sheriff told him.

"Yah? Well, I've got one to make, too. I need to call Betsy. Who you calling?"

"I want to see if Brad had any luck with that APB for Sylvia's car," the sheriff told him.

Both men sat there quietly for a few moments. Finally, Casey said, "To hell with that dog. I'm getting out. Shoot him if he attacks me."

Casey opened the door of the squad car, turned in his seat, and put his feet on the ground. The dog sat and watched him. Casey stood, ignoring the dog, and started walking toward the back of the house. The dog didn't move.

"You forgot the jar," the sheriff yelled.

Casey walked back to the car, opened the back door to get a jar, and the dog jumped into the back seat and lay down.

"Looks like you have company, Sheriff," Casey said.

"Leave the door open and go get that damn sample," the sheriff said.

A few minutes later, Casey was back at the car with a pint jar full of water. Both of the car's back doors were open and the sheriff was trying to coax the dog out of the car.

"He doesn't want to get out," the sheriff told Casey.

"Well, we can't take him with us," Casey said. "Give him a push."

"You give him a push. Every time I try to touch him, he growls at me."

"You got any food?" Casey asked him.

"Do I look like a restaurant?" the sheriff said. "No, I don't have any food."

"How about a ball? We could throw a ball and see if he'll go get it."

"Shut up, Casey."

"I'm just trying to help. Wait. There's a car coming up the drive."

Michael McMillan pulled up in front of his house and parked his Ferrari. He exited the car and looked at the sheriff, with a puzzled look on his face.

"You trying to steal my dog, Sheriff?"

"You're Michael McMillan, right?"

"That's right," Michael replied.

"Then maybe you can get your dog out of my car. He won't budge."

Michael laughed. "He loves to go for rides. He's not going to get out until he's had a ride. I go through this all the time. Just drive him around for a few minutes.

"That's it?"

"That's all it takes. I guarantee it."

The sheriff looked at Michael, trying to figure out if he was pulling his leg. "Casey, take that nice dog for a ride."

"Sure thing, Sheriff. There's nothing I can think of that I'd rather be doing than chauffeuring this here dog around."

Later Monday Afternoon

"Can I get you something to drink? Some water or iced tea, maybe?" Michael asked the sheriff.

"Thanks. I could go for a nice cold glass of water if it's not too much trouble."

"Not at all," Michael said, as he walked over to a wet bar and poured the water. "Obviously, you're here for a reason. It's about Sylvia Toppers, isn't it?

"You knew her?"

"Very well. She was a lovely woman. We dated for a few months, but that ended a while back."

"What's a while back?" the sheriff asked.

"Six weeks – two months. It's hard to remember. Time goes by so fast, doesn't it? It's probably closer to six weeks."

"When was the last time you saw her?"

"Saw her or spoke to her? I saw her last Sunday. We go to the same church and, as I was leaving after the first service, I saw her pull into the parking lot. The last time I talked to her was when we decided to end our relationship."

"Did you end it on friendly terms?" the sheriff asked him.

"Oh, yes. No hard feelings at all. We were just looking for different things in a relationship."

"What would that be?"

"Sylvia liked to play. You know. Have a good time and not get serious. I enjoy a more serious relationship. I'm pretty much a one-woman type of guy. She felt I was pushing her to move faster than she was comfortable with, so we ended it."

"Aren't you still married, Mr. McMillan?"

"No. My divorce was final last week."

"But you were still married while dating Ms. Toppers. Was she uncomfortable with that?"

Michael laughed. "I don't think the status of any man she dated mattered to her. As I said, Sheriff, she didn't want a serious relationship."

"Did she ever mention to you where her money came from? She was quite wealthy, you know."

"Really? Sylvia had money? That's news to me. We never really talked about finances. She seemed to be comfortable, but not rich. She never gave me that impression at all."

"Did Sylvia ever use your swimming pool? By the way, you have a beautiful yard. The view is spectacular."

"Thank you. Yes, we swam together frequently."

"Do you have a pool service maintain your pool?"

"Yes. They come in and service it a couple of times a week."

"Do you know the last time your filter was changed?" the sheriff asked.

"I have no idea. You'd have to ask them."

"I will. What company do you use?"

Sheriff Berkson laughed to himself as he approached the squad car. Casey was sitting in the passenger seat, door open, talking out loud while scratching the dog behind his ears.

"Who's a good boy? You are. That's right. You're a good boy. You like that, don't you?"

The dog was sitting on the ground, his docked tail wagging, and enjoying the attention.

"Looks like you've got a new friend," the sheriff said.

Casey jumped. "Didn't see you coming," he said. "You kinda scared me there, Sheriff."

"Let's head back to the station. I need to make a few phone calls before we call it quits for the day."

"Brad, get me the phone number for Dolphin Pool Service," the sheriff yelled, as he walked into the office.

"I'm on it," Brad yelled back.

"What are you checking, Sheriff?" Casey asked.

"I need to know when the filter was last changed in Mr. McMillan's pool. Hopefully, not in the past couple of days."

"Do they work on Sundays? It probably hasn't been changed, unless they serviced the pool today," Casey remarked.

Officer Brad Herzberg handed the sheriff a piece of paper. "Here's the number," he said.

The sheriff called the number and waited a few seconds for someone to pick up on the other end. "This is Sheriff Berkson, over at the Hollister Police Station. I'd like to speak to the manager, please. Thank you." He waited until a voice on the other end answered.

"Are you the manager?"

"I was wondering if you could check and tell me when you last changed the filter in Michael McMillan's pool."

"Thank you."

"They're checking," he said to Casey.

"Right," Casey replied.

"Yes, I'm still here. Is that right? Requested, did you say? A dead what? I see. Thank you. Bye, now."

Sheriff Berkson sat back in his chair and put his feet up on his desk. "It seems Mr. McMillan neglected to tell us that he called and requested that the pool be cleaned this morning. He told them he found a dead armadillo floating in it. They went right out and serviced the pool, which included changing the filter."

"I thought armadillos knew how to swim. Seems kinda weird to find two dead animals floating in pools today. It's not that hot out."

"I'm not even sure there was an armadillo in McMillan's pool. He told them that, but they didn't see one when they got to his house. Anyway, how about you take that water sample over to Doc Harris? Ask him to check it against the water in Sylvia's lungs. Then go on home, Casey. I'll see you in the morning."

Tuesday Morning

Sheriff Berkson, Deputy George, and Steve Leyson were sitting at Leyson's kitchen table.

"You sure I can't get you a cup of coffee? I just made a fresh pot. It's called Jamaica Brown and it's quite good," Steve said.

"We're fine, Mr. Leyson. I think we've both had our fill of coffee this morning."

"Please, call me Steve."

"I understand you knew Sylvia Toppers, Steve. Can you tell me about your relationship with her?"

"Ah, yes. Dear Sylvia. I was sorry to hear about her drowning. That surprised me, as she was quite a strong swimmer. But accidents do happen, I guess."

"Yes, they do, Steve. Did you have a relationship with her?"

"I guess you could say I did. However, it was a business relationship only. She was a whiz on the computer. I'm not. A four-year-old is better on a computer than I am. I needed a software program for my business, which would be easy to use. She wrote one for me."

"That's it?" asked the sheriff.

"Pretty much. Occasionally, the program needed a little tweak, so we might see each other to discuss how to change it.

Mostly, though, our conversations were on the phone," Steve told him.

"When was the last time you spoke with her?" Casey asked.

"It was weeks ago if I remember correctly. There was no reason to talk to her lately, as everything was running smoothly. Why all the questions, if you don't mind my asking, Sheriff?"

"Sylvia Topper was murdered. We're just following up with some of the people she knew, trying to get an idea of what she had going on in her life."

"That's terrible. Who would want to hurt Sylvia? She was such a nice woman," Steve said.

"That's what we're trying to figure out," said Casey. "Did she ever mention anything about someone wanting to hurt her?"

"Not at all. As I said, I hadn't seen her for some time. Sorry, I can't help you, Sheriff. I hope you get the bastard that did this."

"Casey, you want to get that sample before we leave?" the sheriff asked his deputy.

"I'm on it. Nice meeting you, Mr. Leyson." Casey stood up, shook Leyson's hand, and left.

Steve Leyson had a puzzled look on his face. "What sample is that, Sheriff?"

"We need a sample of the water in your swimming pool. Sylvia had water in her lungs when we found her. We're just trying to rule out that the water came from your pool.

"Don't you need a warrant for that, Sheriff?"

"I don't think so, Mr. Leyson. Do you have a problem with us taking a little sample of your pool water?"

"That doesn't make sense. Didn't she drown in the lake?"

"I never said she drowned, but she was in somebody's pool before she died. We plan on finding out just whose pool it was."

"Well, it wasn't mine. Take all the water you need. Take the whole damn pool, if you want. This is ridiculous, coming in here and trying to pin her murder on me. I'd like you to get the hell out of here."

"I'm sorry if you're upset. We're not trying to pin anything on you. We're just doing our job here. Testing your pool water will rule you out as a suspect."

"Fine. Just leave, please."

Sheriff Berkson got up and left Leyson's house, wondering if he had missed something. Leyson had really lost it when he mentioned the pool. Perhaps, he did have something to hide.

He joined Casey, who was sitting in the front seat of the squad car waiting for him. "Call Funtelli. Tell him I want him to canvass this neighborhood. I want to find out if Leyson had any regular visitors that we should know about."

"Sure thing, Sheriff. Any particular reason?"

"He didn't want to give up his pool water without a warrant. He got real defensive about it. I just figure we should do a little more digging into him, that's all."

"You think Funtelli stopped to see Myrtle this morning?"

"Hell, no. He's gonna avoid that woman as long as I let him."

"How long is that gonna be?"

"Not very long," the sheriff replied.

"Sylvia's sister is coming to town tomorrow. You think we should still search her house again?" Casey asked.

"I do. Call Carlson and tell him to get over there and go through it one more time. I want him to go over every inch of that house from top to bottom."

"What are we looking for?"

"Anything that will give us a clue as to how the hell that woman was half-drowned, choked, and shot to death."

Steve Leyson was so angry he threw his coffee cup against the wall, shattering it. He tried to remember the last time Sylvia had been in his pool. A week ago, maybe? He knew she hadn't gone for a swim the last time she was there.

Anyway, what could they possibly find in that water that could connect him to her? Nothing. That's what. Nothing to be afraid of, anyway. Except, what if they did find something?

After Steve lost his wife, people were always trying to set him up with some friend or relative. Steve didn't want another relationship. For months, after a Ride the Ducks vehicle had run over his wife and killed her, he could barely stand to be around people. His friends didn't give up on him and, eventually, he started accepting some dinner invitations.

Steve had met Sylvia at a St. Patrick's Day party. They hit it off and, when Steve mentioned that he was looking for someone with software experience, she volunteered.

She wrote the program he needed for his business, showed him how to use it, and handed him her bill. He asked her if she would like to go out for dinner and she said yes.

Neither of them wanted to get married again. They enjoyed each other's company and went out every few weeks. The evening usually ended with them in bed.

Now, Steve Leyson was in his kitchen, beating himself up for not telling the truth to Sheriff Berkson. He had just dug a hole for himself, and he didn't know how to get out of it.

Tuesday Morning - Two

Bobby Johnson was living the life of a millionaire, which he was. The least expensive thing he had bought since he had inherited all those millions, was his mobile home. He had gone for the best you could buy, added all the upgrades, and it still cost less than his in-ground pool. He was driving some of the most expensive cars on the market, had a yacht down at the marina, and his own plane. He had all the big boy toys and was still bored.

Bobby had rarely dated until he came into money. Now, he had his choice of women, all eager to share in his wealth. He occasionally brought one home to spend the night, but rarely dated the same woman twice.

Sylvia was the exception. They knew each other before his mother was murdered and his brothers went to jail. He had paid her a million dollars for one little lie, which changed his life forever.

If she had allowed it, he would have swept her off her feet and carried her away. She was his soul mate, but he wasn't hers. He had loved her and now she was dead.

Bobby was in his pool. He had just finished his morning swim and was floating on his back, resting. He wasn't crazy about swimming, but the pool was convenient and the exercise certainly kept him trim. In addition to that, the women loved it. It was almost as good as telling them he had a puppy. They couldn't wait to see it.

He wondered when the sheriff would be back to ask him more questions. Knowing that he knew Sylvia and that he has a pool, probably put him on the sheriff's short list of suspects. After all, Sylvia had testified against his brother, Big John, at the trial, and was the reason he was in jail. The fact that he had dated her would definitely raise the sheriff's curiosity.

Bobby couldn't wrap his head around the fact that he would never see Sylvia again. He knew that she had affairs with numerous men, but they never seemed to last long. Perhaps, a few weeks or months, and then she would get bored and move on. He tried to remember if she ever mentioned some of their names. He doubted that she did. Although they shared a lot, she kept her private life private. He did seem to remember that she mentioned she would only date men with money. He had laughed, when she told him that, as at the time he was broke and living with his mother in her trailer.

They never stopped seeing each other, as friends or lovers. Regardless of her affairs, she always was there for him when he needed her. He was going to miss her. He had lost his best friend and it hurt.

Bobby was sure the first question the sheriff was going to ask was who he had been in bed with, the night Sylvia was murdered. He smiled, picturing the expression on the sheriff's face when he heard his answer.

Tuesday Noon

Chuck Oberson wasn't home. From the looks of his yard, he hadn't been home in a long time. The grass looked like it had not been cut in ages, at least a week's worth of newspapers were on his front porch, and the weeds in his flowerbeds were higher than most of the flowers.

"Looks like nobody's been here for a while," Deputy George said.

"This is the problem with people," said the sheriff. "It's obvious that no one is here, yet the paper boy just keeps throwing the papers on the porch. Why not just hang a sign to let thieves know this house is available to rob? Make a note, Casey, to call the paper and talk to them about this."

"You want me to try the door?"

"Might as well, long as we're here. I doubt anyone's gonna answer, though."

Deputy George got out of the car and walked to the front door. He knocked a couple of times and waited for someone to answer. Then, he knocked again, put his ear to the door, and listened. He turned towards the squad car and motioned for the sheriff to join him.

"What's up?" the sheriff asked, as he approached the door.

"I hear something. It's either someone moaning or a dog whining. What do you think?"

The sheriff put his ear to the door and listened. "I don't hear anything," he said.

Casey knocked hard on the door. "Now I hear it," said the sheriff. "We've got to get in there."

"You want me to break it down?"

"How? You gonna kick it in?"

"I could."

"The only thing you'll break is a bone. Let's check the back door or see if there's a window unlocked."

They found the back door locked, but it had a window, which Casey broke with the butt of his gun. He reached inside the window, unlocked the door, and they entered the house. They followed the sound of whining and found a dog lying in the living room.

"Call animal control and get them out here," the sheriff told his deputy.

"You smell that, Sheriff?"

"You better call the coroner, too," the sheriff answered. "We have a body."

Deputy George and Sheriff Berkson were having a late lunch at Minnie's Diner. They had left after the dog, which was close to death, and the body of Chuck Oberson, who was definitely dead, had been removed from Oberson's house.

"Doc figured he had a heart attack. It's sad about the dog. I wonder if he'll live. It's lucky the door to that bedroom was shut or I figure the dog would have fed off that body. Good thing the air conditioning was on, too or that smell would have been worse. Man, there's nothing worse than a decaying body. Right, Sheriff?"

"Will you kindly shut up? I'm trying to eat my lunch. God, Casey, what's wrong with you?"

"A little squeamish there, Sheriff? Sorry. I didn't know that kind of stuff still bothered you."

"Just show a little respect, okay?"

"I said I'm sorry."

"We've still got Jimmy Johnson to talk to. He's trouble, so be ready for anything."

"And, Bobby Johnson, too. Although, he did say he was with a woman, didn't he?" asked Casey.

"Yes, he did. We need to find out just who that lady friend is."

Jimmy Johnson was in his front yard, working on his pickup truck when the sheriff pulled up and parked the squad car. Jimmy walked towards the car and waited for the sheriff to get out.

"It wasn't me."

Sheriff Berkson grinned. "What wasn't you, Jimmy?"

"Whatever the hell you are here for. It wasn't me and I didn't do it."

"Relax, Jimmy. I just want to ask you a couple of questions."

"What about?"

"You know Sylvia Toppers?" the sheriff asked.

"Sure, I know Sylvia. I've worked on her car a few times. What about it?"

"She's dead, Jimmy."

"Fuck, no," said Jimmy, looking genuinely surprised. "What happened?"

"Someone murdered her. You know anything about that?"

"I know it wasn't me. Damn, Sheriff. I liked her. She was a nice lady. Always treated me with respect, which is a hell of a lot more than you do."

"When did you last see her?"

"It's been a while. Maybe three, four months ago, if I remember correctly. I did an oil change and replaced an air filter. Just regular maintenance."

"Did you two have a relationship?"

"Hell, no. She never gave me a second look and, to tell you the truth, Sheriff, I don't go for older women."

"Did she ever go swimming in your pool?'

"Seriously? Why in the world would she go swimming in my pool? You think she brought her car here and then went for a dip in my pool?" Jimmy asked, laughing. "Sheriff, my old lady would kill me if I so much as looked at another woman."

"You're married?"

"Sure am."

"Who'd you marry?"

"Janie Berg, from Kirbyville. We've been living together for almost a year now. After I knocked her up, I figured I best marry her. I didn't want her daddy coming after me with his shotgun. Her daddy is the one that killed that 700-pound wild boar last year. It was in all the papers."

"I know the family. Is Janie here? I'd like to talk to her," the sheriff said.

Jimmy took a few steps towards his house and yelled, "Janie, honey, would you come out here for a minute"

Janie appeared at the door and yelled back. "Whataya shouting at me for, Jimmy?"

"Sheriff here wants to talk to you."

Janie walked down the steps and joined the three men. "Hi, Sheriff. Hey, Casey. How y'all doing?"

"Hey, Janie. Congratulations on your marriage. I'm just wondering if you can tell me where you and Jimmy were on Sunday."

"Let's see. This is Tuesday. Hey, Jimmy, what did we do Sunday?"

"Don't answer that, Jimmy. Janie, I want you to tell me where you were."

"God, I'm so forgetful. Sorry, Sheriff. This pregnancy has my mind scattered at times. We drove to Joplin on Saturday and spent the weekend with my sister and her family."

"When did you come back?"

"Yesterday morning. We spent Saturday and Sunday there and drove back early Monday morning. What's going on, anyway?" she asked.

"It's nothing to concern yourself with, Janie. By the way, Jimmy, I wonder if we could take a look at your swimming pool?" the sheriff asked.

"My swimming pool? Help yourself."

"Casey, go take a look," the sheriff said.

Casey walked towards the backyard, carrying a pint jar in his hand.

"What's the jar for?" Jimmy asked.

"We need a water sample."

"Sheriff, there's no water in that pool. I broke that pool down last year after the city informed me that I would have to fence the area. I hardly used it, so I emptied it. It's out there in the backfield."

A few minutes later, Casey walked back to the sheriff and stood there with an empty jar in his hand. "Pool's gone," he told the sheriff.

"You done here, Sheriff?" Jimmy asked, with a grin on his face.

"I think we are. Congratulations, you two, and good luck with that little one. It's good to see you're finally settling down, Jimmy."

"Not much choice, right, Sweetheart?" Jimmy said, hugging his wife.

"Well, we'll be off. Thanks for your time."

"Bye, now, y'all," Janie said.

"What you smiling about?" Casey asked the sheriff, as they drove away from Jimmy's house.

"Just amazed at how a woman can change a man. A year ago, Jimmy would have been ready to fight before he answered a question. Now, he's sweetie this and honey that, all over the place."

"I guess we all have to grow up eventually," said Casey. "Having a baby will do that to you."

Tuesday Afternoon

At three o'clock, Sheriff Berkson, Deputy Casey George, Officer Simon Funtelli, and Officer Tim Carlson were in Minnie's Diner, drinking coffee.

"Funtelli," the sheriff said, "Did you find out anything from your canvass in Leyson's neighborhood?"

"You know, Sheriff," Funtelli said, "It seems that every neighborhood has that one old lady who has nothing to do. She lost her husband years ago and has absolutely nothing to look forward to. Her kids are grown, have moved away, and she's lonely. So, you know what she does all day? I'll tell you what she does. She sits in front of her window and spies on her neighbors. She knows every detail of every person who goes in and comes out of every house. She knows every kid on the block and they probably behave a little better, because they know she'll tell their parents if she sees them doing anything wrong. She. . ."

Funtelli, will you just tell me what you found?" the sheriff asked as his aggravation with Funtelli's rant began to surface.

"In every neighborhood, I've ever lived in, there was an old lady like that," Funtelli continued. "But, not Leyson's. Oh, no. There's not one old lady within a four-block radius that saw anything."

"So, you have nothing?"

"I didn't say that. I said there wasn't one old lady. I didn't say there wasn't one old man. Mr. Ben Cason. He might be the greatest witness we could ever have."

"You know I'm going to kill you, don't you?" the sheriff said, trying to be serious.

"He sure got you, didn't he?" said Carlson, laughing.

"Here's what I found out," said Funtelli, getting serious. "According to Mr. Cason, once or twice a week, a silver Toyota Camry was parked in front of Leyson's house. It was always the same woman driving the car and, from his description, it was most likely Sylvia."

"How's his vision," asked Casey.

"He's pretty sharp and I would say his vision is good. It seems that her visits have gone on for quite a few months, mostly at night. He said it wasn't unusual for her car to still be there in the morning, so it looks like she was spending nights with Leyson."

"Could he recall the last time he saw her car parked at Leyson's?" Casey asked.

"He saw her car there Friday night."

"Not Saturday or Sunday?" the sheriff asked.

"Not that he could recall," Funtelli answered.

"Carlson, did you find anything at her house that we overlooked the first time?"

"I went through that house from top to bottom. No secret hiding places, that I could find. I found a few fingerprints and Brad is following through to see if we can determine who they belong to. I would probably guess they're Sylvia's. Her place was pretty clean and looked like it had been dusted recently."

"Did you find a calendar?" the sheriff asked. "According to Brad, there wasn't one on her computer or phone."

"She had a calendar on her refrigerator. I think she had one on her desk, too. I should get those," Carlson said.

"I think you should. That's it then. Go back up there, Carlson, get those calendars and take the tape down. Her sister will be here soon and I don't see any problem with her staying there," the sheriff said.

"Did Brad get any leads on the car?" Casey asked.

"Nothing. It seems everyone and his uncle drive a silver Camry. Hopefully, it will turn up soon."

"What has Doc Harris got to say about the water samples?" Office Carlson asked.

"Haven't got his complete report on that yet," answered the sheriff. "He hasn't sent his final autopsy report to me, either. Remind me to check on that, Casey."

"More coffee, anyone?" the waitress asked, interrupting the conversation.

"Thanks, no. We're good," the sheriff told her. "All right, guys. Let's get back to work. Funtelli, did you stop and see Myrtle this morning?"

"Sorry, Boss. No time, with all the canvassing and stuff going on."

"You were supposed to talk to her first thing this morning before you did all that stuff that's going on."

"I'll catch her tomorrow. I promise." Funtelli said.

"You'll catch her today," the sheriff responded.

"Come on, Sheriff. You know she isn't going to know anything. I doubt she'll even remember we were there on Sunday. It's a huge waste of my time."

"Time you're getting paid for."

"She hits on me."

"What?"

"She hits on me," Funtelli repeated. "She makes me nervous."

"Tomorrow morning, Funtelli. You show up there tomorrow morning and question her. And, then the next day and the next, and so on, until this case is solved. I don't think she's quite as dimwitted as she makes out to be. I have a feeling she saw something and perhaps, just perhaps, it will come floating to the surface one of these days."

"She wants donuts," Funtelli told him.

The sheriff laughed. "So, take her a dozen donuts. Maybe they'll help her memory."

"Who's gonna pay for them? I'm sure not buying her any damn donuts."

"I'll reimburse you," the sheriff told him, while Casey and Tim broke up laughing.

"Casey, will you head over to Mr. Leyson's house and ask him to join us over at the station? We need to have another talk with that man."

"Sure thing," Casey replied.

The four men walked across the street to the police station. Before they were even through the door, Brad was yelling at the sheriff. "We got her car. It was parked on the side of the road up on State Highway T."

"Who found it?" the sheriff asked.

"A woman called the Branson Police and told them that a car had been sitting on the side of the road for a couple of days. They checked and saw we had an APB out on it. They're having it towed in right now."

"Are they bringing it here, Brad?" the sheriff asked.

"Yes, Sir. They're doing us a favor." Brad responded.

"Well, that's one mystery solved. I'm heading over to pick up Leyson," Casey said

"Be careful Casey. I don't trust that one, the sheriff said.

Late Tuesday Afternoon

Bobby Johnson and Cynthia Hughes were lying on matching lounge chairs, next to Bobby's pool.

"Tell me about Sylvia," Cynthia said.

"I really don't want to talk about her," Bobby said. "Besides, there's nothing to tell. She was a neighbor, we were friends, dated for a while, and we broke up."

"That's it?" Cynthia asked. "I thought you two were serious."

"Whatever gave you that idea?"

"Your brother. Big John told me that you two were super tight."

"Cynthia, that's ridiculous. I didn't even date her until after Big John went to jail. Why would he even say that?" Bobby asked.

"I think he is trying to figure out why she lied about seeing his truck, at your mom's house, the night she was killed. He swears he wasn't there and he thinks you got her to lie."

"When the hell did he say that? Are you visiting him in jail?"

"I see him from time to time. After all, we're engaged. I'm gonna help him with his appeal. I don't think he did it. I think I would have known if he had left the house that night."

"You were knocked out by that sleeping pill. You said so yourself."

"Well, yeah. But I don't think he did it."

"It had to be him. We know Tom didn't do it. His alibi is tighter than a virgin. If it wasn't Big John, who else could it be?" Bobby asked.

"You."

"What the hell, Cynthia? Why would you say that?"

"Well, Bobby, you're the only one left. Like you said, who else could it be?"

"Cynthia, my love. You are way off base. One more dip before we shower and head out for dinner?"

"No, thanks. I think I'm just gonna close my eyes for a few minutes. That sun feels so nice on my body."

"And, a nice body it is," Bobby responded.

Cynthia closed her eyes and drifted off. As Bobby watched her sleep, he wondered what the hell Big John was doing. If he was working on an appeal and was gonna try to pin this on him, he better watch what he said to Cynthia. Perhaps, it would just be better if he quit seeing her altogether. Too bad, he thought. She really is great in bed.

A little over a year ago, an attempt had been made to kill Bobby's mother. The first shot missed hitting her, but the bullet entered her trailer and lodged in the refrigerator door. The second shot took out her little toe.

A few weeks later, Tom, Bobby's younger brother, after a night of drinking with friends, came home and found his mother's dead body. Somebody had broken into her home and smothered her with a pillow. Tom had an ironclad alibi and was not a suspect in her murder. However, shortly after her death, Hook, the town drunk, was arrested for public intoxication. He drunkenly confessed, to the sheriff, that Tom had hired him to shoot his mother. Tom was promptly arrested for attempted murder and put in jail.

At the time, Cynthia and Big John were engaged and living together. Cynthia could not swear that Big John was home and in bed, the night of the murder. She had taken a sleeping pill and slept soundly. Although Big John was a suspect, there was no physical evidence against him. Then, a neighbor, Sylvia Toppers, went to the sheriff and disclosed that she had seen Big John's truck, at his mother's house, the night she was murdered.

Hook, who had lied about Tom, was now living on an island in the Caribbean. A sweet old lady, named Joyce, who lied to provide Bobby with an alibi, was enjoying her remaining years in a high-rise condo in Florida. And, Sylvia lied about Big John's truck being at his mother's house the night of her murder.

Now, both Tom and Big John were serving sentences in jail for crimes they didn't commit, and Sylvia was dead.

Tom would be locked up for another fourteen years. Perhaps, he would get out in six and a half, but it was based on good behavior, and Tom found it hard to hold his temper. Big John, on the other hand, was looking at spending the rest of his life in jail.

Bobby believed he would never have to worry about Hook, Joyce, or Sylvia. He had paid them handsomely and they had been grateful. He knew Hook would never come back to the states, much less Missouri. He had left the country before his trial and there was an outstanding warrant for his arrest.

He was confident that Joyce would never talk. He was concerned, though, that if Big John did get an appeal for a new trial, she would be called back to testify. Perhaps, she would have to leave the country, also.

It gave Bobby no satisfaction, knowing there was one less witness that could pin him to his mother's death. He already missed Sylvia and the thought that he wouldn't see her again was heartbreaking.

He sometimes wondered if it was worth losing his family for a few million dollars. He smiled to himself, almost laughing out loud. It was worth every stinking penny, he thought.

He glanced at Cynthia and wished it was Sylvia lying there. Yes, he thought. Cynthia has to go. Tonight will be our last night together.

As Bobby slowly drifted into the same nothingness as Cynthia, his last waking thought was that he was sure he was going to hell.

Even Later Tuesday Afternoon

Sheriff Berkson looked questioningly at Officer Tim Carlson. "Well?"

"What?" Carlson replied.

"Is the car here yet?"

"I didn't hear you ask me that. Did you just ask me that?"

"Tim, has Sylvia's car been dropped off yet?"

"Yeah. The forensic guys are going over it right now. There's blood in the back seat."

"Any fingerprints?"

"Don't know," Tim replied. "All I heard is that there's blood in the back seat."

"Casey," the sheriff yelled. "get Doc Harris on the phone."

Casey dialed the Doc's office and got a message that he could not come to the phone right now. "Not answering," he told the sheriff.

At the same time Casey hung up the phone, Doc Harris walked into the police station, carrying a large envelope.

"Just trying to call you, Doc," the sheriff told him. "You got a report for me?"

"You know, Cowboy, you're very impatient. You want everything yesterday. You've been in this business long enough to know that these things take time."

"Sorry, Doc. This thing with Sylvia is getting to me. I don't like it when people die on my watch. Anyway, whatcha got?"

"There's not much that you don't already know. There was alcohol in her blood, but she wasn't drunk. She went through hell before she died. I figure her head was held under water first, accounting for the water in her lungs. She managed to bring a lot of it up. The choking came next, but it didn't kill her. The shot in the forehead did her in. She also had bruising, which indicates she was either hit with an object or kicked. I'll put my money on being kicked."

"Was she sexually assaulted?" the sheriff asked.

"I would say no. No signs of bruising or tearing in that area, but she did have sex sometime that day."

"You got a DNA sample?"

"I do. Now I just need someone to match it to," the Doc replied.

"Did you want to say something, Casey?" the sheriff asked.

"We should get samples from McMillan, Leyson, and Bobby Johnson. We know she was sleeping with all of them, at one time or the other. There might even be more we don't know about yet."

"We'd need warrants," said the sheriff. "And, we need some evidence to get them."

"You got the water test results back, yet, Doc?" Casey asked.

"I do. None of them is conclusive. The closest match is Leyson and that's stretching it."

"Anything that would hold up in court?" the sheriff asked.

"Nothing. I wouldn't even try. A defense attorney would make mincemeat out of me if I so much as suggested there was a match."

"What's your best estimate for the time of death?"

"I would say between midnight and two a.m. Sunday morning. I don't think she was in the water for more than six or seven hours."

"So, we don't have anything more to go on than we did before," the sheriff stated.

"Except for the DNA. That might help if you can find a match," Doc Harris said.

"Thanks, Doc."

"Let me know if there's anything else I can do," the Doc said, as he left the police station.

"Let's go take a look at that car," Sheriff Berkson said to his deputy.

An hour later, Olivia Frankel walked into the Hollister Police Station.

Sheriff Berkson did a double-take, thinking he was seeing a dead person walking.

Deputy Casey stared at the woman, mouth open, dropped his cup of hot coffee onto his lap, and yelled.

"Sorry, about my deputy, Miss. You must be Sylvia's sister, Mrs. Frankel."

"Good afternoon. Are you Sheriff Berkson?"

"Yes, ma'am. Sorry about your loss. I see you found us okay. Have you been out to the house yet?"

"No. You're my first stop. I don't have a key. I figure you must have a key, so I can get in."

"Of course. This is Deputy George. Casey, get the key for Mrs. Frankel."

"Please, call me Olivia."

"So, you and Sylvia are twins. She told me she visited you down in Texas, but she didn't mention you were identical twins."

"We're not. I'm two years older."

"Well, you could certainly pass for twins. Will you be staying at her house while you're here?"

"If that's not a problem with you. I'm not planning to stay long. The family wants Sylvia put to rest back down in Texas. As soon as arrangements have been made to fly her back, I'll be leaving."

"That's not a problem. We're done with her house. It's fine for you to stay there. We'll be glad to help you with whatever you need. Doc Harris, the coroner, has completed his autopsy. There's no reason why you can't take your sister back to Texas with you."

"I'd like some details of what happened here. Needless to say, we're all very upset, losing her like that."

"Mrs. Fr - Olivia. Believe me, we are doing everything in our power to find out who did this. Deputy George will go over everything with you. He'll catch you up to date."

Casey walked over to Olivia and took her arm. "Please, ma'am, come with me. Can I get you a cup of coffee or something else to drink?"

"You look like you wet yourself, Deputy. Would you like to clean up before we start?" Olivia asked, grinning.

Wednesday Morning

Officer Funtelli got out of his squad car. The sheriff may think this is funny, but I sure as hell don't, he thought. Knowing he had to talk to Myrtle was making his stomach churn. Just do it, he muttered to himself and took a couple of steps towards the bait shop. He stopped, walked back to the car, opened the door, and got back in.

He took a donut out of a box and took a bite. It was jelly-filled and delicious. He finished eating it, never taking his eyes off the bait shop. He couldn't see who was inside the building. Perhaps, Myrtle wasn't there. Maybe just Jake was working this morning. He reached into the box and took out another donut. It was gone in three bites.

"Screw this," he said. He grabbed the box of donuts, got out of the car, and walked to the bait shop.

"Morning, Officer."

Funtelli jumped. "Christ, you scared me, Jake. Where did you come from?"

"Saw you sitting over there. Wondered when you were gonna get up the guts to come over here," Jake said, laughing.

"Sorry, Jake. She scares me."

"Hell, Funtelli. She scares everyone. Even me. But I love her, such as she is."

"Is she here? Sheriff says I need to keep questioning her."

"She's down on the dock. Why don't you just leave those donuts and tell the Sheriff she wasn't here? That's not really a lie. She's over there, so she's not here."

Funtelli laughed. "Has she said anything more about Sunday morning?"

"I don't think there's anything else to say. She saw the body and she pulled it in. Hell, Funtelli. She didn't see anything. This is a waste of your time. But we sure do enjoy getting donuts. Hope you got a few jelly ones in there."

"I ate a couple, but there's still ten left," Funtelli told him, as he handed Jake the box.

"Sounds good to me. You doing this every morning?"

"Until the sheriff closes the case."

"Mix it up a little, will you? I love jelly donuts, but wouldn't mind if you throw in a couple of Boston Creams now and then."

"Got it. Thanks, Jake."

"No problem."

Steve Leyson hadn't been home yesterday when Casey stopped by to pick him up. It didn't look like he was home now, either. Casey knocked again. No answer. He stepped off the front porch and walked around the house to the backyard. He looked through the back door window. Nothing looked disturbed.

As Casey walked back to his squad car, he noticed an elderly man waving at him. He waved back. The man motioned for him to come over. Casey walked to the other side of the street.

"What can I do for you, sir?"

"You looking for Leyson?"

"I wanted to speak to him. It seems he's not home, though."

The old man shook his head. "No sir, he sure isn't. He threw a suitcase in his car and took off."

"When was that, sir?"

"It wasn't too long after I talked to that officer," Ben Cason said.

"That would be Officer Funtelli?"

"Yes, sir. That's his name. Funtelli. Maybe an hour after he left, Leyson drove off."

"And, you haven't seen him since?"

"As far as I can tell, he hasn't been back home. Didn't see no lights on in his house last night. Nope. He's gone. You think he did it? You know, kill that nice lady?"

"Right now, Mr. Cason, we have no idea who killed Ms. Toppers. If you see Mr. Leyson, would you give us a call? I'd certainly appreciate any help you can give us."

"Don't you worry none, young man. If I see anything going on over there, I'll give you a call."

"I appreciate it," said Casey.

"Her calendars tell a story," Officer Herzberg told the sheriff. "A lot of initials, but it's pretty obvious who they are."

"Whataya got?"

"A lot of days marked with SL, BJ, and MM. There are a few with the initials WW."

"Who's WW?" asked the sheriff.

"No idea. We know she was seeing Steve Leyson, Bobby Johnson, and Michael McMillan, but I have no idea who WW is."

"Steve Leyson is lying about the last time he saw her. What does her calendar tell you?"

"She has him down for Friday night. That agrees with what old man Cason told Funtelli."

"Saturday night?" the sheriff asked.

"Michael McMillan. He told us he hadn't seen her for about six weeks or so. He was down for the 24th, but she crossed him off. Before that, she has him down for the 2nd. Looks like both him and Leyson were lying."

"So was Bobby Johnson, if BJ is him."

"Probably is," Brad replied. "He's all over her calendar."

"So, what we have here are three men who all said they were no longer dating her, who are lying through their asses."

"Looks like it, Sheriff."

Sheriff Berkson turned to see who was coming through the front door. "Hey, Casey. Where's Leyson?" the sheriff asked.

"He's gone. His neighbor, that old guy Funtelli talked to, told me he threw a suitcase in his car and took off."

"When was that?"

"A few hours after we talked to him. Whataya thinking?"

"Brad, let's put an APB out on Mr. Leyson. No telling what he's up to. Meanwhile, Casey, I think we should go visit Bobby Johnson and Michael McMillan again. They've got some explaining to do."

"I sure would make our jobs a lot easier if people just stopped lying," Casey said.

"Keep dreaming," replied the sheriff.

Wednesday Morning - Two

"I'm telling you, I hadn't seen Sylvia for at least six weeks. I have no reason to lie."

"Mr. McMillan, we have information that you were with her on Saturday night."

"What information?"

"Can you tell us where you were from nine o'clock Saturday night until six o'clock Sunday morning?" Sheriff Berkson asked.

"Of course, I can. I was here, at home, all night."

"Were you alone?"

"I was. I watched a little TV, spoke to a couple of people on the phone, went for a swim, checked my email messages, and went to bed," he replied.

"Do you recall who you spoke to?" the sheriff asked him.

"I spoke to my sister, who lives in Illinois, and to a business acquaintance."

"Isn't it unusual to be doing business late on a Saturday night?" the sheriff inquired.

"Not for me."

"When we inquired about your pool, why did you neglect to mention that you had just had the filter replaced that morning?"

"It was? I didn't know that. I requested that they clean the pool because I found a dead animal floating in it. If they changed filters, well, then, that's news to me."

"You didn't think it might be important to tell us that the pool had been serviced that morning?"

"If I recall correctly, Sheriff, you didn't ask me that. You asked when the filter had last been changed. I didn't know it had been changed that morning."

"You enjoy playing games, Mr. Leyson?"

"Not at all. Now, if there's nothing else, I'd like. . ."

"When was the last time you saw Sylvia?" the sheriff asked again.

"To be honest, Sheriff, I don't really know. It seems like at least six weeks ago, but maybe it wasn't that long."

"Maybe more like four weeks?"

"Possibly," McMillan replied.

"Maybe you were with her on Saturday night?"

"Absolutely not, and if anyone says I was, they're lying."

"What if I told you that the water in her lungs matches the water in your pool?"

"Then, I would have to say you are lying. Now, Sheriff, if there's nothing else, I'd like you to leave."

"You know it's against the law to lie to the police, don't you?" the sheriff asked.

"So, arrest me for having a bad memory," McMillan retorted. "If you had any evidence that I was with Sylvia on Saturday night, we wouldn't be standing here talking. You would have already arrested me."

"One more thing, before we leave, Mr. McMillan. What day of the week is your garbage picked up?"

"On Thursday. Tomorrow. Why?"

"So, if I go take a look in your garbage, am I going to find a dead armadillo?"

"I guess you'll never find out, Sheriff. My garbage container is in the garage, and you'd need a search warrant to take a look"

"What do you think?" Casey asked the sheriff, as they drove away from his house.

"I think he's lying through his teeth," the sheriff answered. "Call Brad and tell him I want a warrant issued to search McMillan's house. We have cause. He lied to us and he's impeding an investigation. We need to go through his phone and computer. Let's see if he made those phone calls and was on his computer late Saturday night."

"What about his garbage?" Casey asked.

"His garbage is going to be picked up tomorrow. I'm gonna have one of my officers riding on that truck."

"Who?"

"I think maybe Funtelli might enjoy riding in a garbage truck for a few hours."

"But he'll miss seeing Myrtle," Casey laughed.

"Oh, I think he'll still be able to fit that in sometime tomorrow. Now, let's go see what Bobby Johnson has to say for himself."

The sheriff parked in front of Bobby's house. "What's missing?" he asked Casey.

"His big ass truck. I don't see it."

"It might be in the shed, with his cars. Let's go see if he's home or not."

Sheriff Berkson and Casey got out of the squad car and walked up to Bobby's front door. Casey knocked, and they waited to see if Bobby would answer the door.

"No one's home," said Casey.

"Try again," the sheriff told him.

As Casey was about to knock again, the door suddenly swung open and they were face to face with Cynthia Hughes. Except for the extremely small bottom of a bikini bathing suit, Cynthia was naked. Her hair was wet and her nipples were hard.

"Why, hello there, Sheriff. Is that Casey with you? Hi, Casey. Haven't seen you guys since Big John's trial. Y'all looking for Bobby?"

85

"It looks like we caught you at a bad time."

Cynthia smiled a big smile. "I just got out of the pool and was about to take a shower."

Sheriff Berkson glanced over at Casey, who was staring at Cynthia's breasts. "Casey, would you go get my pen? I think I left it in the car."

"Why, Sheriff, I've got a pen here in the house I can give you. Why don't you two come on in?"

"Is Bobby home?" the sheriff asked.

"He just went to town to get a few groceries. He'll probably be back in an hour or so. You sure are welcome to wait."

"Thanks, but we'll come back later. Looks like you need to get in that shower and warm up a little."

Cynthia glanced down at her nipples and laughed. "It doesn't take much to get these little puppies hard. That happens every time I get out of that pool."

Sheriff Berkson smiled. "There is one question you might help us with before we leave. Can you tell me where you were Saturday night?"

"Sheriff, is he okay?" Cynthia asked.

Sheriff Berkson glanced back at Casey. "For crying out loud, Casey, take a breath," he yelled. "What the hell's wrong with you?"

Casey looked at the sheriff, glanced at Cynthia again, turned, and walked back to the squad car.

"Sorry about that, Cynthia. It seems your breasts have the ability to put him into some kind of a trance."

"Not the first time, if I remember correctly," she laughed.

"So, where were you Saturday night?" the sheriff asked again.

"Saturday night? I was here with Bobby. All night and most of Sunday."

"How long you been seeing him?"

"A few months. First, we just kinda hung out, missing Big John and all. I guess one thing just led to another."

"How's Big John doing?" the sheriff asked.

"Not real good. I mean, like, how good does anyone in jail do? We're hoping for an appeal, but that takes time."

"I always had my doubts about it being him that killed Melissa, but we had a witness to place him on the scene," the sheriff told her.

"Yeah, you did. And, now that witness is dead. Which is the worst thing that could have happened to Big John's appeal."

"Tell Bobby I stopped by. I'll talk to him later."

"Sure thing, Sheriff. Bye, now."

Sheriff Berkson started to walk back to the car, turned, and looked back at Cynthia. "I may be out of line here, but you have, without a doubt, the most beautiful breasts I have ever seen."

Cynthia smiled and closed the door.

Wednesday Noon

"The blood in the car is Sylvia's."

"We figured it would be," said the sheriff.

"We got a partial print off the inside of the back door. Forensics doesn't think that it's good enough to get a match. They also found some white fiber on the back seat, which they sent to the FBI lab, in Quantico, for analysis. We'll probably hear back in a week or so."

"Can't speed it up any?" asked the sheriff.

"That is speeding it up. Sorry, it's the best they can do."

"I feel like I'm running in circles. Our best suspect, Leyson, left town and we can't find him. Bobby lied about not seeing Sylvia, but he has an alibi."

"Only if Cynthia is telling the truth," Casey commented.

"True. But, when we showed up at his house Sunday morning, he asked if we wanted to wake the woman up in his bedroom. And, this morning, she pretty much confirmed that she was that woman."

"God, she's gorgeous," Casey remarked. "Have you ever seen tits like those?"

"I thought you were going to stroke out. What it is about you and boobs?"

"It's not boobs, Sheriff. It's only her boobs. I just want to bury my face into them and. . . "

"Okay, that's enough," the sheriff said, laughing. "I get the idea."

"My wife would kill me if she heard what I just said," said Casey.

"And, I'd swear you had it coming. Now, getting back to business," the sheriff said, "What do you think about McMillan?"

"I think he's a lying sack of shit. If Sylvia's calendar is accurate, he saw her on Saturday night. He just might be our guy."

"Do we have any idea who WW is?

"Not a clue. Brad's still working on the emails and phone calls. Maybe, he'll find something."

"Well, tell him to work faster. I want this case closed," said the sheriff.

Two hours later, Brad handed the sheriff a list of phone calls that Sylvia had made for the past two months. "I color-coded the calls of interest. Yellow is Bobby, green is Leyson, and pink is McMillan. She spoke to all of them on a regular basis."

"Who's the blue one?" the sheriff asked.

"That is Walter White. He's probably the mysterious WW on her calendar. I checked him out. He lives in Branson, on Lake Shore Drive. Does he have a swimming pool, you ask?

Yes, he has a swimming pool. He's not married. He was, but he lost his wife in a boating accident back in 2001."

"I remember that," said the sheriff.

"He's a doctor. A plastic surgeon and extremely well off. You're gonna like this part, Sheriff. He was arrested twice for domestic violence. The charges were dropped, though, so no convictions. Guess, old WW has a temper."

"You might say that," replied the sheriff. "Thanks, Brad."

"Walter White, huh?" said Casey. "That name sounds familiar. We gonna pay him a visit?"

"We are," answered the sheriff. "Go gas up the car. I'll get his office address and see you back here in a few."

"Wait. It's Wednesday. Aren't most doctors off on Wednesday?"

"Years ago. When was the last time you saw a doctor, Casey? Now, they work six days a week. It's all about the money."

Dr. Walter White was an extremely distinguished-looking man of about fifty. He was thin, tall, and starting to go bald. He held out his hand to Sheriff Berkson, who shook it.

"I won't take much of your time, Doctor. We're investigating the death of Sylvia Toppers. You did know her, right?" the sheriff asked.

"I know—knew her. She is—was a patient of mine. Sorry, I can't wrap my head around the fact that she is gone. Such a lovely woman. I can't believe anyone would hurt her."

"So, she was a patient of yours. Can you tell me the last time you saw her, Doctor?"

"Of course. Just let me check her records"

The sheriff watched while the doctor opened a program on his computer. After entering a password, he typed in Sylvia's name and a new screen appeared.

"Ah, here it is. I saw Sylvia on the 10th."

"Of this month?" the sheriff inquired.

"That's correct." Doctor White responded.

"How long has she been your patient?"

"I first saw Sylvia on April second. Actually, Sheriff, I met her before she was a patient of mine. We met at a St. Patrick's Day party."

"What was she seeing you for?"

"I'm not supposed to reveal that information, you know. Patient-doctor stuff. However, I don't think she would mind if I told you. It was just moles."

"Moles?" Casey said.

"When I first met her, I noticed that she had a large mole on her neck. I mentioned to her that I could remove it without leaving a scar. She asked me for a card and a day or so later, she made an appointment. It turned out that she had several moles that she wanted removed."

"Did she have any other appointments scheduled?" the sheriff asked.

"Let's see. She had one for last Monday, which she missed. Oh, how sad. She was dead and I didn't even know. That was her last scheduled appointment."

"Did you ever see her socially, Doctor?"

"You mean like date?"

"Yeah, like date."

"Oh, my no.

"Guess that's it then. Thank you for your time, Doc. Sorry to have interrupted you during working hours."

"No problem. I'm glad I could help, such as it was," the doctor replied.

"One last thing, Doctor White. Do you usually solicit business while attending parties?"

"Of course not. Just what are you getting at?"

"Think about it."

Dr. Walter White was completely satisfied that he had told the police exactly what he thought they should know. It was none of their business if he had dated her or not. He had thrown them a bone when he told them that he was seeing her to remove some moles. He could have made them get a search warrant. However, that seemed to satisfy them, and he was pleased he had offered the information to them.

He went to a new page in her file and studied the pictures that covered the screen. God, she had been beautiful. He traced her body with his finger, feeling himself getting aroused. He laughed a little, thinking of how she believed he had to take those nude photos for her medical records. It hadn't bothered her at all while she stood there naked, as he snapped a dozen pictures.

Getting as close as possible to her body, while taking close-up photos of her moles, he brushed up against her naked body several times. He shuddered, thinking of how he had enjoyed those moments.

Now, as he looked at those pictures, he felt a slight twinge of regret. He should have been more patient with her. He would have sworn she came on to him at that party, but when he asked her for a date, she had politely refused. Sorry, I'm not interested, she said. I'm seeing someone right now. I'm flattered. I'd love to have you as a friend. Blah, blah, blah. Didn't she know what a catch he was? He was a doctor, for god's sake. A plastic surgeon. He could do miracles. He could turn the ugly into the beautiful.

He smiled. I played that just right, too. I accepted her refusal graciously. There are plenty of women out there who want me. I can have anyone. Except her. I couldn't have her.

Casey and the sheriff were quiet on the ride back to the police station. As Casey parked the squad car, the sheriff said, "I can't put my finger on it."

"On what?"

"Something is off with that doctor."

"You mean like he was lying? I got the impression he was putting on an act."

"He knew she was dead, didn't he? He acted all surprised, but he knew."

"He has this weird look about him," Casey asked.

"It's his eyes," Sheriff Berkson, exclaimed. "It's like they're dead. No, more like vacant. Like nobody's home."

Wednesday Afternoon

"Ben Cason just called," Officer Herzberg told the sheriff. "He wanted to let us know that he saw lights on in Steve Leyson's house last night."

"So, he's home. Tell Carlson to get on over there and bring him in. He's got some explaining to do."

"Yes, sir. I'm on it."

"Where do you think he went?" Casey asked.

"If I knew where he went, I wouldn't have put an ABP out on him, would I? If he was running, though, he changed his mind."

"Sheriff, how many crazy people do you think live around here?" Casey asked.

Sheriff Berkson looked at him for a second, wondering what made Casey ask that question. "All of them," he replied. "I seriously doubt anyone is completely sane, including you and me. I think everyone is a little nuts. It's just that some are more nuts than others."

"Yeah," replied Casey. "Those are the ones we deal with, I guess. The ones that are more nuts."

"How about running over to Minnie's Diner and bringing us all back some fresh coffee and one of her peach pies?"

"I just made a fresh pot of coffee," Casey said.

"And, a fine job you did making that coffee, except it tastes like tar. Dump it out and get someone to wash that pot."

Officer Carlson and Steve Leyson were laughing as they walked into the police station. "That's a good one," Carlson said. "You'll have to tell the sheriff that joke."

"Hey, Sheriff," said Leyson. "I hear you been wondering where I was."

"I figured you skipped town. Guess I was wrong, 'cause here you are."

"I'm frequently out of town, Sheriff. On business. I have no reason to skip town, as you put it."

"It just seems strange that you took off right after we talked to you."

"I don't recall anyone telling me not to leave town. You could have tried calling me, you know. I would have told you where I was and saved you all that aggravation."

"I never said I was aggravated," the sheriff said.

"Just saying, that's all," said Leyson.

"Have a seat. I have a couple of things I'd like to clear up."

"Sure thing. Have you found out who killed Sylvia, yet?"

"When was the last time you saw her?" the sheriff asked him.

"About that. I didn't exactly tell you the truth before. I've been kicking myself ever since. I don't know what came over me and I'm sorry. I saw Sylvia last Friday night."

"Were you having an affair with her?"

"I guess you could call it that. She did do some work for me after we met at a party. That was the truth. Then we just kinda fell into this relationship. We'd get together every week or two and spend a little time together."

"What party was that?" the sheriff inquired.

"One of my friends had a St. Pat's party. I'm not really much of a party guy, but I decided to go. That's where I met Sylvia, and—well, like I said, we just hit it off."

"How serious was it between you two?"

"I wouldn't call it serious at all. We just enjoyed each other's company. I certainly wasn't serious."

"Did you know she was seeing other men besides you?" the sheriff asked Leyson.

"It wouldn't surprise me, but we never discussed it. Sylvia was very private."

"If you had known that, how would that have made you feel? Angry?" asked the sheriff.

"No. Not angry. Probably more careful. You never know who has what these days."

"How often do you go out of town on business?"

"It's usually a couple of times a month. It depends on the time of year."

"You're a suspect in this case, Mr. Leyson. Everyone who knew Sylvia is a suspect right now. However, you lied to us. So, in my eyes, that makes you a bigger suspect than everyone else. I don't want you to leave town again. I can make sure that happens if I arrest you for lying to the police and impeding an investigation. In fact, I can't officially keep you here, unless I do arrest you"

"Please, Sheriff. I am sorry I lied to you. I didn't mean to impede anything."

"I want your word that you'll stay in town until I get this mess settled. If you take off again, I'll throw your ass in jail. Is that clear?"

"It's more than clear. Believe me, Sheriff, I had nothing to do with Sylvia's death. I would never hurt her."

"Maybe. Maybe not. Just stay around, hear?"

"I promise," Leyson replied.

"Officer Carlson will give you a ride back to your house. If you think of anything that might help, give us a call."

"Yes, Sir. I'll be in town. You can count on that."

"Tim, take Mr. Leyson home."

"On it, Sheriff. You gonna save me a piece of that peach pie?"

"If you want some, you better get it now. No guarantee it will be here when you get back."

"Excuse me, Mr. Leyson," Officer Carlson said, as he walked back to the sheriff's desk and picked up the rest of the pie. "I'll just take this with me if you don't mind," he told the sheriff and walked out the door, pie plate in hand.

Sheriff Berkson laughed. "I'm outta here," he said to Casey. "Time to call it quits. Is Funtelli here?"

"He's in the back," Casey replied.

"Hey, Funtelli, get in here," the sheriff yelled.

Officer Funtelli peaked around the corner, at the sheriff. "You want me?" he asked.

"Get in here. Did you see Myrtle this morning?"

"I saw Jake. Myrtle wasn't at the bait store. I gave him the donuts. He told me Myrtle and him talked about finding Sylvia and she don't remember anything more."

"Try again tomorrow."

"Ahh, Sheriff. It's a waste of time. She don't know nothing."

"First, though, before you make your visit to see Myrtle tomorrow, you're gonna go for a ride on a garbage truck."

Funtelli looked at the sheriff, wondering what the hell he was talking about. "What did I ever do to you, Sheriff? You hate me or something?"

"I need you to hop on the truck that picks up Michael McMillan's garbage. Once it's outta his garage, it's ours for the picking. We need to see if there's a dead armadillo in it."

"You want me to bring it to you, if I find one?" Funtelli asked, grinning.

"Bring the whole bag," said the sheriff.

"You want me to bring you a dead armadillo, that's been dead and rotting since Sunday?

"Now that I think about it, Funtelli, I want you to get all his garbage. You can sort through it here, while we watch."

"Casey," Funtelli said, "why does the sheriff hate me?"

"Not sure, bro. I think it just might be that you are so damn handsome."

Thursday Morning

"I'm serious, Cyndi. I think it's best if we stopped seeing each other."

"Big John doesn't have to know, Bobby. I'm sure not going to tell him we've been sleeping together."

"That's only part of it. It's what you said about me killing my mom. How can you be with me if you think I'm a murderer? Better yet, I can't be with you knowing that's what you think of me."

"Bobby, you know I was joking. Besides, that was two days ago."

"It was yesterday, Cyndi. I'm sorry. I just can't stop thinking about what you said."

"You stopped thinking about it long enough last night to screw me," Cynthia said.

"A mistake."

"Damn right it was a mistake. Mine, for even thinking we could be together. You're no Big John, that's for sure," she yelled.

"Stop the dramatics, Cyndi. It's not like we're in love. We had fun for a few months and now it's over. It's time to move on. Just finish dressing and go home. I'll get your things together and drop them off at your place tomorrow."

"Like hell, you will. I'll take my stuff now, if you please. I don't want you touching my stuff."

"Fine. Take your time. I'm going for a swim."

"I hope you fucking drown in that pool," Cynthia screamed at him, as he walked out the door.

As he looked out his kitchen window and saw the garbage truck pull up, Michael McMillan smiled. So much for that idiot sheriff and his threats, he thought. In a few hours, those black bags will join a million others, just like them, at the dump.

His smile faded when he saw the garbage man remove the black bags from his garbage container, carry them to the passenger side of the vehicle, open the door, and place them inside.

Michael made a mad dash for the door, hoping he could stop the truck before it took off down his driveway. He was too late. All he saw was the rear end of the vehicle, as it made its way back to the street.

He went back into his house, slamming the door behind him. Furious, over what had just transpired, he picked up a glass figurine and threw it across the room. It landed on his plush carpet, unbroken. He picked it up, went outside, and threw it again. It landed in his pool and sunk to the bottom, still in one piece. He shook his head in disgust, went back into his house, punched 911 on his cell phone, and waited while it rang.

"911. What is your emergency?"

"I want to talk to Sheriff Berkson. Now," he screamed into the phone.

"What is your emergency, sir?" the voice asked.

"I told you. I want to talk to the sheriff," he yelled.

"Sir, if this is not an emergency, I need to ask you to call back on our non-emergency number. We need to keep this line open for emergencies. Do you have that number?"

"I want to talk to the sheriff."

"Who is calling, please?"

"Tell that asshole sheriff of yours that Michael McMillan wants to talk to him," Michael said.

"One moment, please."

Michael tapped his foot nervously while waiting for the sheriff to pick up his phone.

"I'm sorry, sir. The sheriff said you should call back on the non-emergency number. Do you have that number, sir?"

"Tell him to go fuck himself," Michael screamed, as the connection was lost.

Two minutes later his phone rang

"What?" he yelled when he answered it.

"Mr. McMillan?"

"Yes."

"Mr. McMillan, this is Deputy Casey George from the Hollister Police Department. I was wondering if you could tell me when and where you met Ms. Toppers."

"Is Sheriff Berkson there? I need to talk to him."

"I'll see if he's available. First, however, could you answer that question for me?" Casey said.

"What difference does it make? She's dead."

"Yes, Sir, she is. And, we are trying to solve her murder. Could you answer the question, Mr. Millan?"

"I met her on March 17th at a party. Now, let me talk to the Sheriff."

"I'm sorry, he just left the building. I'll give him a message that you would like to talk to him."

Steve Leyson considered himself lucky. He could be sitting in jail right now. He had lied and he supposed he had impeded an investigation. However, he had cleared the air with the sheriff, and it seemed everything was okay for now. He had been concerned about the pool water, but that hadn't even been mentioned. He figured it was a moot point anyway, as he had told the whole story about him and Sylvia. Well, almost the whole story.

Sylvia hadn't been at his house on Saturday night. That didn't mean he hadn't seen her. It just meant he hadn't seen her at his house.

I guess it's still lying when you purposely omit a fact or two, he thought. Lying by omission, he remembered his minister calling it. Well, tough. There's also some law, or something, that says you don't have to incriminate yourself.

Dr. White backed his BMW 6 Series 640i xdrive out of his three-car garage. He hit the remote to close the garage door and checked to be sure that his cell phone was on. He glanced at his GPS and decided he was good to go.

His receptionist had cancelled all his appointments for the next two weeks. He was feeling stressed and he knew, from past experience, what would come next if he stayed that way. His mother was the only person who could calm him down. He needed to see his mom in Florida.

Five minutes later, he thought he already felt better. Just knowing he would be away from his problems, for a couple of weeks, lightened his mood. Seven minutes later, he took a deep breath and smiled.

Ten minutes later, as he reached to open the moon roof, an oncoming car drifted into his lane, hitting his car head-on.

Officer Brad Herzberg hung up the phone. A lab assistant from Quantico had called and informed him that the results, of the fiber found in the car, were in.

He speed-dialed the sheriff on his cell. "What's up, Brad?" the sheriff said, as he answered his phone.

"Quantico called about that fiber."

"That was fast. They said it would take over a week."

"Seems like it's a pretty common fiber," Brad said.

"So, what is it?"

"It's a cotton terrycloth fiber, usually found in high-end robes," Brad said. "That fiber came from a very expensive white terry cloth bathrobe."

"Thanks," said the sheriff, and ended the call.

Later Thursday Morning

"For god's sake, Funtelli, do that someplace else. You're stinking up the whole office."

"Sheriff said to go through it. Didn't say where," Officer Funtelli replied.

"Well, he sure as hell didn't mean here," said Deputy Casey. "Take that crap out back."

"Just look at all this stuff," Funtelli said. "He must not cook much. Lots of carry-out containers and pizza boxes. Hey, here's a dead cat. It looks like it's been chewed up a bit. This is where the stink is coming from."

"Probably his dog caught it. He has a Doberman. Sweet thing. Likes to ride in cars," Casey said. "You find an armadillo in there?"

"No. It looks like the cat is the only dead animal in these bags. Looks like McMillan was lying about finding that armadillo floating in his pool."

"Funtelli, what the hell you doing?" the Sheriff yelled, as he walked into the office.

"No armadillo, Sheriff. Just a dead cat," Funtelli said.

"Get that crap out of here. What's wrong with you, anyway, bringing that stuff in here?"

"Sorry about that. I'm going. Do you want I should sort out the mail and letters? It looks like he cleaned out his desk or something. There's a lot of paper in these bags," Funtelli said.

"Sort through all of it. There's something in there he didn't want us to see," said the sheriff.

"Will do," replied Funtelli.

"What did Myrtle have to say this morning? Did she remember anything?" the sheriff asked, with a big grin on his face.

"Myrtle wasn't there this morning. Just Jake. He sure is enjoying all those donuts."

"Myrtle's always there. That's two mornings now you claim she wasn't there. What's going on?"

"No idea."

"Maybe you should stop by later today and check again. Best be sure she's okay."

"Come on, Sheriff. Twice in one day? You must have better things for me to do."

"Actually, I do. We're gonna pick up that search warrant and go through McMillan's house. You're coming with us."

"What about the garbage?"

"You can finish that later."

"No way, I'm letting you in," Michael McMillan shouted.

"Mr. McMillan, we can do this the easy way or the hard way. It's up to you. But we're coming in. I have a search warrant. And, I want your phone."

"You're not getting my phone. I know my rights."

"This search warrant gives me the right to take your phone, computer, and anything else I want. I suggest that you take your dog for a walk while we get busy," the sheriff said.

"Get off my property."

"Officer Funtelli, would you please handcuff Mr. McMillan and put him in the back of the squad car?"

Funtelli walked over to McMillan, cuffs in hand, and politely asked him to turn around. "No way you're cuffing me," McMillan screamed.

"You really want to resist?" Funtelli asked, threatening.

McMillan looked up at the six-foot-six-inch deputy and shook his head no. Funtelli slapped the cuffs on his wrists, walked him to the squad car, and shoved him into the back seat.

"Give me your phone," Funtelli said.

"I'm not giving you. . ."

"Now. Or, I'll take it from you," Funtelli interrupted.

McMillan took his phone out of his pocket and handed it to the officer. "You all think you're so smart. You'll be hearing from my attorney. This is harassment."

"Just doing my job, sir," Funtelli replied, smiling.

Two hours later, the van pulled away from McMillan's house and headed to the police station. It was carrying various items removed from McMillan's house, which included a laundry basket filled with dirty clothes, two computers, and files from his office. A woman's hairbrush had been placed in a forensic bag to be analyzed. McMillan's toothbrush was also collected, in order to obtain a DNA sample.

Michael McMillan watched as the three policemen exited his house. Sheriff Berkson walked over to the squad car, opened the back door, and told McMillan to get out.

"You're not arresting me?" McMillan asked.

"Not right now. You'd just be another prisoner that my wife has to cook for and she's not feeling that well. Don't leave town, McMillan. If you try, I'll haul your sorry ass in and make sure the judge doesn't set bail."

"You can't do that," McMillan said.

"Sure, I can. Wanna try me?"

"Walter White was in a car accident this morning," Officer Herzberg told the sheriff.

"The doctor we talked to?" Casey asked.

"Same one. He was hit head-on."

"How bad was it?" the sheriff asked.

"Bad, but he'll live. It looks like he was leaving town. He had a packed suitcase in his car."

"Where'd it happen?" Sheriff Berkson asked.

"On Cliff Drive, right before you get onto 65. Looks like he was heading south," Brad answered.

"Let's run another check on him. There may be more to Dr. White than we thought."

"I'm on it. Oh, you'd never guess what they found in his car."

"I'm not in the mood for guessing games this morning, Brad. Just tell me."

"It seems Dr. White might have had the hots for Sylvia Toppers. According to Deputy Sheridan, he had a bunch of nude photos of her with him."

Sheriff Berkson didn't say anything for a few seconds, thinking about what he had just heard. "Brad, how well do you know Sheridan?"

"We're buds. We play on the same baseball team. I've known him since we were kids. Why?"

"Give him a call. Tell him that Dr. White is a suspect in Sylvia Toppers' murder and we would appreciate it if he would send us copies of those photos."

"Why, Sheriff, you old dog. What would Sarah say if she caught you looking at nude pictures of Sylvia?"

"Will you grow up? Also, ask him if they found anything else in the suitcase or car that looks suspicious. Then call Judge Peterson and get us a search warrant for White's office and house. I think we should find out what the doctor was up to."

"You think she was messing around with him, too?" Brad asked.

"If she was, that makes three we know of so far. We need a sample of his DNA. Take care of that, will you?"

"Maybe four, if Bobby Johnson was still seeing her."

"Bobby's out of the picture. He has a pretty solid alibi."

"Cynthia," Brad said, factually.

"Yep, Cynthia," echoed the sheriff.

Around Noon on Thursday

Dr. White didn't feel right. Slowly his memory brought him back to the last thing he remembered, which was the impact to his car. He opened his eyes and looked around the room. He was in a hospital room. Then the pain kicked in and he moaned, getting the attention of a nurse who was standing at the end of his bed.

"Welcome back. I'm Caroline, your nurse. Of course, you know that, seeing as how we both work here. We were wondering when you were going to open those big eyes of yours. You're having some pain, I guess. Well, don't you worry none about that. Caroline's gonna make it all go away."

Dr. White didn't say anything. He watched her walk over to the side of his hospital bed and push a button. Morphine, he thought. Almost immediately, the pain subsided and he was out.

Caroline stood there and smiled as she watched him close his eyes and sink into nothingness. "Hope you have a good sleep, you pecker head," she whispered. She checked his vitals and left the room.

Officer Tim Carlson watched Nurse Caroline as she left Dr. White's room. He took a few big steps and caught up with her at the Nurses' Station.

"Morning. I'm Officer Carlson, with the Hollister Police Department. Is that Dr. White's room that you just came out of?"

"Morning, Officer Carlson. Yes, that's his room."

"I need to get a DNA sample from him."

"Just what would you be needing a DNA sample for? Has he done something wrong? Please, tell me he's in trouble with the law."

"Whoa, there. I didn't say that."

"No, but if you're looking for a sample, he must have done something wrong."

"We have several people we need to eliminate as suspects in a case we're working on. Dr. White just happens to be on that list. As far as I know, he's not in any trouble. My boss sent me over to get a sample."

"Your boss that guy they call Cowboy? I know him. He's a real nice fella."

"He's great. So, it's okay if I go swab his cheek?"

"It's okay with me. I'm not sure if it would be okay with him, though. You have a warrant?"

"I can get one real fast if it's a problem with you," Officer Carlson said.

"No problem with me. Go knock yourself out."

"What you said – about him being in trouble. What did you mean by that?"

Caroline gave Carlson a long, hard stare. After a few seconds, she sighed. "I can't stand that man. He's a pig. This hospital has lost some really good nurses because of him. I came close to leaving, but no high and mighty doctor is gonna get rid of me that easy. He used to get too friendly with me, but I brought a grievance against him and he was warned to lay off."

"So, the doc's a lady's man?"

"No, Officer Carlson. He thinks he's a lady's man. What he is is a pig. Always leaning in too close and trying to cop a feel with the nurses. I could handle that, but when he slipped his hand down the back of my slacks and rubbed his finger between my cheeks – well, let's just say I lost it."

"No wonder you don't like him. Sorry you had to go through that."

"I spoke up. He left me alone after that, but he still tries that crap with some of the nurses. Usually, it's the younger ones who are too afraid to say anything."

"It doesn't look like he'll be getting fresh with anyone for a while," Carlson said.

"Not with his right hand anyway," said Caroline. "It was crushed in the accident. His career is over and I'm not one bit sorry for that asshole."

"How serious is his condition?"

"It's not good. A couple of broken ribs, a ruptured spleen, and some internal bleeding. He'll be going in for more surgery this afternoon.

"You want to take the swab for me?"

"I'd be happy to," replied Caroline. "Follow me."

Sheriff Berkson and Deputy George were sitting at their desks looking at the pictures of Sylvia.

"She was truly a beautiful woman," said the sheriff. "It's a shame what happened to her. She must have really pissed someone off."

"She was seeing Dr. White to have some moles removed, right?" asked Casey.

"That's what he told us. Why?"

"Look at these pictures. I see a mole on her neck. That must be the one the doctor mentioned to her at the party. Then, there's one above her right breast and one on her back."

"That seems about it," replied the sheriff.

"Why all the nude pictures? Why not just take pictures of the moles? Did he have to have all these naked pictures to remove a couple of moles?"

"Good point, Casey. We have the warrants to search his place. Let's see if he took nude pictures of all of his patients or just the good-looking ones. Has Tim come back with that swab yet?"

"He's on his way back with it. He called a few minutes ago. He had a conversation with one of the nurses who works at the hospital. She told him White is a real pervert. She called him a pig. Said she brought a grievance against him a while back."

"I knew there was something about that man I didn't like," said the sheriff.

"So, are we heading over to search his office now?" Casey asked.

"No. Tim and Zeke can do that this afternoon. We've got other things to take care of. Have you heard if Sylvia's sister has left town yet?"

"Haven't heard a word from her since the first day she got here. I imagine it's a lot of work to make arrangements to take a body back home with you," replied Casey.

"Just wondering, that's all. Been wondering about that St. Patrick's Day party, too. It seems that's where Sylvia met White, McMillan, and Leyson. Who the hell threw that party, Casey?"

Thursday Afternoon

"She wouldn't talk to me."

"Whataya mean, she wouldn't talk to you? You said she has the hots for you," the sheriff said, laughing.

"I brought her donuts today, too, just like every day."

"Every day, Funtelli?"

"Almost every day. Anyway, she said she was busy and she'd see you later."

"See me?" the sheriff asked. "Why does she want to see me?"

"I don't know, Sheriff. You know she doesn't make any sense half the time. All I know is that she said her and Jake will see you later," Funtelli answered.

"Was Jake there?" the sheriff asked.

"No. Just Myrtle this morning. She saw me drive up, ran out to the car, and told me she would see you later."

"Did you tell her to come see me, Funtelli? Because, if you did, I swear to god I'll put you on garbage patrol for the next ten years."

"I didn't do nothing. I swear. I don't know what's going on with that woman."

"Thanks a lot. Now I have that to look forward to for the rest of the day," the sheriff groaned.

"Wouldn't have happened if you didn't make me go there every day," Funtelli muttered.

"What's that? You got something to say?"

"Nothing," Funtelli said, as he walked away.

Olivia Frankel stood on the sidewalk, in front of the police station, watching the sheriff and his deputy walk out of the diner and cross the street.

"Afternoon, Ms. Frankel," the sheriff said. "You coming to see me?"

"Afternoon. I'm leaving to go back home in a few hours. Fisher's Funeral Parlor has been wonderful helping me with all the arrangements."

"Again, I'm sorry for your loss. Is there anything I can do?" the sheriff inquired.

"I'd like to leave you a key, just in case something comes up. I had a duplicate made. I'll be back up in a few weeks or so to list the house with a realtor. I thought I'd have an estate sale. There are a few things I want to keep, so I'll probably drive up next time."

"I'll be happy to keep an eye on the place for you," the sheriff said.

"I found something that you might want," Olivia said. "It may not mean anything, but it might help."

"What would that be?" the sheriff asked.

"A recipe box."

"I'm a little confused," said the sheriff. "How would a recipe box help?"

"I'm sorry," Olivia said, laughing. "Not the box. It's what's in the box. Sylvia was a sentimental person. She liked to keep mementos of places she went, things she did, and things that were important to her. This box didn't hold recipes. It held postcards, invitations to parties she'd been invited to, and some letters and notes from special people. Things like that."

"That might help us. That the box you holding?"

"It is. Like I said, I don't know if anything in it will help you, but I thought you should take a look at it."

Olivia handed the small recipe box to the sheriff. "I'd like it back someday when you're finished with it," she said.

"I'll take good care of it, Olivia. Don't you worry none. You have a safe trip home. We'll see you in a few weeks."

"Bye, Sheriff. Officer George. Take care, now."

The sheriff and his deputy watched as Olivia drove off. Sheriff Berkson looked at Casey and said, "How the hell did we miss that box? We searched that place more than once and it was right in front of our eyes."

"I'll go through it. We don't know if there's anything in it that'll help us."

"That's not the point. We overlooked something in plain sight."

"It's a recipe box, Sheriff. Recipes are supposed to be in there, not all that other stuff."

"Even so, I must look like a fool in that woman's eyes."

"Let's go inside," said Casey. "I'll check it out."

Casey spent a few minutes sorting the items in the box. There were postcards from friends, some thank you notes from her nieces down in Texas, and a few old invitations. As he started to write a list of names of people to check out, he picked up one of the old invitations. "Son of a bitch," he exclaimed. "Hey, Sheriff."

"What?" asked the sheriff.

"I know who threw that St. Patrick's Party."

"You have the invitation there?"

"I sure do. Rachel Hammertoe threw that party."

"The queen of high society, here in Hollister?"

"The one and only," replied Casey.

"Well, guess that answers that question. I think we should pay Ms. Hammertoe a visit. I want to see that complete guest list."

"You ever been in her house?"

"I'm not considered one of Hollister's elites. So, no. I've never been invited to her house."

"There are less than 4,500 people in Hollister. How many can possibly be considered elite?"

"I'm sure there's a handful. Maybe Michael McMillan and Dr. White would fit into that group."

"White is from Branson. He doesn't count," said Casey.

"Well, Leyson's from here, and I sure don't see him being in that elite crowd. Wonder why he was invited to one of her parties," said the sheriff.

"You want to drive over to see her now," Casey asked the sheriff.

The sheriff let out a loud groan, and muttered, "She's here. God help me."

Casey looked towards the door and laughed when he saw Myrtle walk in, carrying a plastic bag. A second later, Jake joined her, out of breath.

"Slow down, will you?" Jake yelled at Myrtle.

"If you quit those damned cigarettes, you wouldn't be out of breath all the time," Myrtle said.

"I don't smoke anymore, Myrtle. I quit twenty-five years ago," Jake said.

"Really? Seems just like yesterday I saw you smoking."

"Wasn't me, Myrtle."

"Well, then, maybe you should quit buying all those damned donuts. You're fat. That's probably why you're out of breath."

"Hey, Sheriff," Jake said. "How y'all doing?"

"Hey, Jake. Myrtle. What's going on?"

"Myrtle fished this out of. . . "

"Let me tell him," Myrtle interrupted. "I found it. I should be the one to tell him. Hi, Cowboy. Where's that handsome policeman you got working for you?"

"Officer Funtelli is out on an assignment right now, but I'll tell him you asked after him. So, you got something to tell me?"

"I found this here plastic bag. Somebody threw a perfectly good piece of clothing away. I was gonna wash it and keep it, but Jake said I had to give it to you. Said it might be evidence. He figured we should ask you before I kept it. So, you think I can keep it?"

"Let me see the bag, Myrtle. Then, I'll let you know if you can keep whatever's in there."

Jake took the bag from Myrtle and handed it to the sheriff. "It's a robe, Sheriff. A nice one."

The sheriff opened the bag and took out a white terrycloth robe. He glanced over at Casey and said, "Looks like this could be where that white fiber came from. Take this to forensics and see if it's a match."

"I don't get to keep it?" Myrtle whined.

"Sorry, Myrtle. It might be evidence in a murder case. We do appreciate you and Jake bringing it to us. You did the right thing. Where did you find it?"

"It just washed up out of the water."

"She found it resting up against the dock," Jake said. "This morning early, about 6:30. I figure it would have sunk if it hadn't been tied up in that bag."

"Well, you have no idea how much this helps us, Jake. We need all the help we can get figuring this one out."

"You talking about that Ms. Toppers who was murdered?" Jake asked.

"That's the one. Thanks for bringing it in?"

"I found it," said Myrtle. "Is there a reward or something?"

"Sorry, no reward."

"That sucks," she said. "How about you get that handsome policeman to bring us some donuts? We like the jelly-filled ones."

"You just told me I was fat from eating donuts," said Jake. "Now you want some more."

"Hell, Jake. No one said you had to eat them."

Rachel Hammertoe

Rachel Hammertoe spent the morning on the phone. She was planning a luncheon. This is when she was at her best. She loved the excitement of surprising her guests by serving them exotic meals. She had invited nine of her closest friends which, including herself, would make ten at the luncheon. She made sure her tables were always set for an even number of people.

She knew they would all show up. No one ever missed one of her affairs. Everyone knew if they turned down an invitation, it would be the last time they would be invited.

She was positive that most of them had never heard of, much less eaten, the items she had chosen from the menu. It would start with a traditional Mulligatawny soup, a choice of Lamb Mango Curry or Shrimp Kashmiri for the main course. There would be a variety of vegetables and, of course, Mango Kulfi ice cream would be served as dessert. The servers would be dressed in dhotis and saris. Dancers would be a nice treat, she thought. She must check to see if there was somewhere she could hire Indian dancers.

It made no difference what the cost was, as money was no object to Rachel. By the time she was done paying for this luncheon, the bill would be at least five figures. That meant that each meal would be close to a thousand dollars. You didn't find real Indian food in Hollister or Branson and the caterers were being flown in from Chicago. They just better be worth it, she thought.

Rachel tried to entertain at least once a month, and the number of guests varied depending on her mood. Months with holidays were her favorite, as she could work around a particular theme. She was famous for her New Year's Eve parties, which usually ended sometime on January 2nd.

The door chime startled her and brought her back to reality. Wondering who could be visiting this time of day, she waited for her maid to announce the visitor and to ask if she was receiving.

The chime rang again. Rachel waited in her den for the maid. Then, it chimed again. She became irritated that her maid, who she was paying good money to do a job, was not answering the door. She walked to the front door and opened it.

"May I help you?" she inquired.

"Afternoon, ma'am. I'm Sheriff Berkson from Hollister. This here is Deputy Casey George. I'm wondering if I could speak with Mrs. Hammertoe."

"May I inquire what you wish to speak to her about?"

"Is she in, ma'am?"

"I'm Mrs. Hammertoe. What do you want, Sheriff?"

"I have a couple of questions I was hoping you could help me with. May we come in?"

"Of course. Sorry, I'm distracted. I don't understand why my maid didn't answer the door. I don't usually answer the door. I didn't mean to be rude. Please, come in."

"We'll just take a few minutes of your time," said the sheriff.

Rachel led them into a large sitting room and asked them to sit. "What can I possibly help you with?" she inquired.

"I understand you threw a St. Patrick's party a few months back. I'd like to see your guest list."

"What on earth for? That seems a strange request to me. I wonder where that girl has gone off to now."

"Excuse me?"

"Sorry. I don't know where my maid is. I know she was here this morning."

"Yes, ma'am. So, about that list – do you have a copy you can give me?"

"What's this all about, Sheriff?"

"I understand that Sylvia Toppers attended a party you threw here on St. Pat's Day. She was a guest, is that correct?"

"Oh, my. Dear, sweet Sylvia. I heard someone murdered her. Who would want to hurt that sweet girl? It's terrible, just terrible, isn't it?"

"Yes, it is. We're trying to find out who did this to her. I understand that she met a number of men here at that party. We were wondering if we could have a copy of the guest list."

"You think someone from my party killed her?" Rachel asked.

"We need to explore all the possibilities. This is just one area that we're checking up on."

"Of course, of course," said Rachel. "I'll do whatever I can to help. Wait here a moment. I'll see if I can find that list."

Within the minute, Rachel was back in the room holding a leather-bound book about the size of a small photograph album. "Here's the guest list for that party. I prefer not to part with my book. Would it be alright with you if I copied it and emailed it to you?"

"Mrs. Hammertoe, how about we take it back to the office and make a copy of those pages on our copy machine? Casey here will bring it right back to you. Would that be alright with you?"

"You promise you'll bring it right back? I need it, you see, for my next party?"

"I promise," answered the sheriff. "I appreciate your help."

"Of course. You can let yourselves out. If you see that maid of mine, will you send her in here?"

"Just one other question, ma'am."

"Yes, Sheriff. What would that be?"

"How come you invited Steve Leyson to that party? He doesn't seem to fit in. I mean, he doesn't impress me as having a lot of money. You understand what I'm asking, ma'am?"

"Of course, I do. I'm rich. He's not. Why would I want someone like him attending one of my affairs? It's simple. My niece asked me to ask him."

"I see. Well, then, that answers that. Just who would your niece be?"

"Cynthia Hughes. I believe you've met her. She was engaged to that horrible man who murdered his mother."

"Big John Johnson," the sheriff said.

"That's the one."

"Thank you, again."

"I'm going to fire that girl if I ever find her."

"Yes, ma'am," said the sheriff, as he and Casey started to leave Rachel's house.

Suddenly, the sheriff stopped in the doorway. Casey, right on his heels, bumped into him. "Sorry," Casey muttered.

"Mrs. Hammertoe, what about Sylvia Toppers? Why did you invite her?" the sheriff asked.

"Sylvia? My niece asked me to invite her, too. I guess, in a way, Cynthia and I held that party together. About half the people who attended were her guests. Between you and me,

Sheriff, quite a few of them were not my kind of people, if you know what I mean."

"Yes, ma'am, I believe I do. Thanks again for your help."

"I'll expect that book back within the hour, Sheriff,"

"Yes, ma'am."

Later Thursday Afternoon

They made it to the squad car before Casey started laughing. The sheriff looked at him, trying to keep a straight face, with absolutely no luck. By the time the two of them were inside the car, they were laughing hysterically.

"So – that's – Rachel Hammertoe," Casey managed to say, trying to catch his breath.

"I'm proud of you, Casey," said the sheriff. "You managed to hold it together."

"Only because I didn't open my mouth and say anything," Casey replied. "I knew I'd lose it if I did."

"Well, now we know how the makeup companies stay in business," said the sheriff.

"Perfume people, too. I don't know what she was wearing, but it sure cleared out my sinuses."

"How old do you think she is?" Sheriff Berkson asked.

"Hard to tell. Probably eighty, trying to look forty. If her face was stretched any tighter, her ears would be meeting in the back of her head."

"Well, meow," laughed the sheriff.

"Yeah, maybe. But, it's true."

"Tell the boys I'm having a "go over" meeting at four. I want all of them there."

At four o'clock, the sheriff and all his officers were sitting around a large table in Minnie's Diner. They all ordered coffee and a piece of pie, except Funtelli, who told the waitress to throw a scoop of vanilla ice cream on his.

"Do you really need that ice cream, Funtelli?" the sheriff asked.

"Have to keep up my strength, Sheriff. Besides, you're paying."

"I'm paying for the pie and coffee. You're paying for the scoop of ice cream."

"Hey, Beverly," Funtelli yelled, "make it three scoops on that piece of pie."

"Alright, let's get down to business. Everyone settle down. Funtelli is not funny. Never has been. So, Brad, what have you got from the lab?"

"The fiber from the car matched the fiber from the robe. It was expensive. I only found one store in the area that sells that brand. It's a high-end store in Springfield, called *Class It Up*. It's an extremely popular item. They've sold about a dozen in the past year to people here in Hollister. Six were purchased by Michael McMillan, four by Bobby Johnson, and two by Steven Leyson."

"Steven Leyson spent that kind of money on some robes? That seems a little rich for his blood," said the sheriff.

"The manager of the store was extremely helpful. When I talked to her, she mentioned that Leyson acted like he was hesitant to spend that kind of money. He commented that his lady friend enjoyed swimming and loved wearing that particular robe after she got out of the water."

"What kind of money are we talking about, Brad? How much could a robe cost?"

"Those robes cost over $400.00 each," Brad answered.

"Holy shit," said Casey. "Who would spend that kind of money on a dumb old robe?"

"Someone who could afford it, I guess," said Brad.

"Or, someone who was trying to impress a lady," commented the sheriff.

"Right," said Casey.

"Zeke, find out if these guys still have all the robes they bought. If they refuse to show them to you, we'll get a warrant. Hell, we already searched McMillan's. Brad, were any robes found?"

"I'm not sure," said Brad. "I know they took his dirty laundry. I'll find out if any were in there."

"Well, let's hope someone is missing one. What else, you got?"

"The fingerprints on the car were unusable."

"We already knew that," said the sheriff. "What else?"

"We have McMillan's DNA off his toothbrush. We should get the results pretty soon and know if that was his semen. Same thing with White. We should hear soon."

"Did we get a sample from Leyson yet?"

"Nope. Maybe Zeke can manage to get one when he goes over there to check out the robes?" said Casey.

"Good idea. Zeke, get a swab from him. If he hasn't got anything to hide, he'll let you take one."

"I'm on it, boss."

"Don't call me boss," said the sheriff. "Is that it? Good lord almighty, we haven't got diddly poop here, guys. We need to catch a break. Brad, you and Funtelli get that warrant and get White's house and office searched. We still need to find out what he was into. Maybe he was just a pervert, but who knows? I don't give a damn, right now, about patient/doctor confidentiality. Bring in those computers. Check to see if he had any of those white robes. Check everything. Under sinks, behind furnaces, and in cracks. I don't want anything missed. Understood? I don't want another screw-up like the one we had with Sylvia's house."

"What happened?" Funtelli asked.

"Did you enjoy that ice cream?"

"Sure did. What screw-up?"

"We missed a recipe box sitting on the counter in the kitchen. It had some information we were wondering about.

We would have found out anyway, but it was a little embarrassing when Ms. Topper's sister brought it to us."

"Sorry, I missed that," said Funtelli, grinning.

"You keep that shit up and next time it'll be your leg that Myrtle ties a rope to. Casey, you copy that guest list?"

"Sure did. Mrs. Hammertoe was real happy when I returned her book."

"Did she ever find her maid?" the sheriff said, laughing.

"Well, no. But, for a good reason. Seems Thursday is her maid's day off," answered Casey.

"It must be hell to grow old. That's about it then," said the sheriff. "We've got three persons we are looking at. Leyson, McMillan, and White. We still need to find out why Cynthia Hughes wanted Leyson and Sylvia at the party. I didn't know that the two women knew each other, except from the trial. So, why would she invite Sylvia? Maybe, through Bobby? Check to see if he was at that party, Brad. He dated both of them. Right now, we've got more questions than answers, guys. Let's get this closed. It's been almost a week."

Cocktail Hour

As Bobby Johnson dressed for the evening, he thought about the past few days. He missed Sylvia. Much as he hated to admit it, he had loved her.

He wondered what Sylvia had been into. Although they kept in touch and spoke often, she was a private person and shared little of her personal life with him. She did mention meeting a man at a party who, after only a few dates, had asked her to marry him. She had laughed when she told him that and said it was too bad that men always ruined a good thing by bringing up marriage. He tried to remember if she had told him his name. It didn't come to him.

Then, there was that doctor who removed a mole from her neck. She said he creeped her out a little. He kept calling and asking her out and got angry when she said no.

Damn, he thought. If I had just pushed a little, maybe she would have told me who these guys were. I really miss her, he thought. She was my last true friend and now she's gone. Bobby wiped a tear from his eye. Man, he thought, I've got to stop feeling sorry for myself.

He picked out the shoes he would be wearing for the evening and sat down to put them on. His mind changed gears and he focused on Cynthia. He knew dating Cynthia had been a mistake. She was fun, but he didn't trust her. He couldn't figure her out, either. He knew she was still in love with his brother, Big John, but had no qualms about screwing him. Bobby figured she was playing him, trying to get information that would help get Big John out of jail. Yes, he was better off without her.

He looked at himself in the mirror, satisfied with what he saw. He may not be the best-looking guy in town, but he was one of the richest. Women will take money over looks any day of the week, he thought.

He punched a number into his cell phone. It was answered on the first ring. "Get the plane ready. I'll be there in fifteen. And, Steve, make sure Annie has a pitcher of margaritas ready."

"Hollister Police Department," Officer Herzberg said, as he answered the phone.

"Sheriff Berkson there?"

"One moment. Who's calling?"

"Bobby Johnson."

"Hold on."

Bobby continued driving to the airport, hoping he was doing the right thing. Just as he had pulled out of his driveway, a name had popped into his head.

"Sheriff Berkson, here. What can I do for you, Bobby?"

"This may not be news, but I just remembered something that Sylvia told me a few weeks ago."

"What would that be?"

"Did you know that Michael McMillan asked her to marry him?"

"She told you that?"

"She did. She told him no, though. She didn't want to see him after that. He was getting too serious."

"That's it?"

"I guess. She did tell me that a doctor she had seen kept bugging her for a date. He got pretty upset when she kept turning him down."

"That would be Dr. White?"

"Never gave me his name. Just that she had gone to him to have some moles removed."

"That's White. Why are you just telling me this now, Bobby?"

"The name just came to mind. Thought you might like to know, that's all."

"Thanks, Bobby."

"See ya, Cowboy."

"Well, I'll be a monkey's uncle," said the sheriff.

"What was that all about?" Casey asked.

"It seems Sylvia refused McMillan's offer of marriage. That probably pissed him off. He has quite a temper and it doesn't take a lot to set him off."

"Well, that could be a motive. She rejected him. He wanted to get even."

"Could be. She rejected White, too. Seems he was pretty upset when she refused to date him."

"Upset enough to kill her?" Casey asked.

"Who the hell knows, Casey? I've been doing this job for a long time, and it still amazes me what sets people off."

"She sure had a lot of guys who had the hots for her," said Casey.

"She certainly did. I wonder what was so special about her."

"Well, for starts, she was a very pretty lady. She had a great figure. Nice boobs, if I remember correctly."

"As nice as Cynthia's?" the sheriff asked, grinning.

"Don't even go there," said Casey.

"Her sister is nice. Maybe she was just a real nice lady. I guess we'll never know now."

"Did I mention that we got the ballistics report back?" Casey asked.

"The shell came from a .45, right?"

"Yep. We didn't find a gun in McMillan's house. Maybe, White or Leyson has one."

"Zeke back yet?" Sheriff Berkson asked.

"Just walked in a few minutes ago."

"Call him in here,"

Casey walked to the back of the room, stuck his head through a door, and told Zeke the sheriff wanted to see him.

"You coulda just yelled," the sheriff told Casey.

"You want me, Sheriff?" Zeke asked as he walked into the room.

"What did you find out?"

"Leyson hasn't got any white robes. He did give me a swab, though."

"Where are they? Did he say?"

"Get this. He returned them. Said he never used them, so he returned them and got his money back."

"Check that out first thing tomorrow morning," the sheriff said.

"Right. McMillan could account for four of the six he bought. Says he doesn't know where the other two are. I checked the garbage we brought in. They are not in there. Bobby Johnson wasn't home."

"I just talked to him," said the sheriff.

"Doesn't mean he was at home."

"Right. Check him out tomorrow, too."

"Does Leyson own a gun?" the sheriff asked.

"He's a hunter, so I figure he does," answered Casey. "Just don't know what kind or how many. You figure we should get a search warrant for him, too?"

"No cause to get one. At least, not yet. Well, boys, I'm done for the day. I'm going home, have a few cocktails with Sarah, and enjoy a home-cooked meal."

"You're so lucky, Sheriff. My wife can't cook for shit. I'd trade her for Sarah any day," said Casey.

"There's more to life than food, Casey. Just quit complaining and be thankful for what you've got."

"Amen, to that," said Zeke.

Cynthia Hughes

The banging on her front door woke Cynthia out of a deep sleep. She glanced at the clock and swore, wondering who the hell was waking her up at 6:30 in the morning. She threw on a robe and stumbled to the door, ready for battle.

"What the hell do you want?" she yelled, as she opened the door. "Do you have any idea what time it is?"

Officer Tim Carlson, hat in hand, smiled and said, "Yes, ma'am. I certainly do. Sheriff Berkson sent me on over here to ask if you would join him at the station. He has a few questions he would like to ask you."

"You go tell Cowboy that he can go to hell. I'm going back to bed."

"Sorry, ma'am. I have strict orders to escort you to the station. Perhaps you'd like a few minutes to get dressed."

"Are you fucking deaf? I just told you I'm not going anywhere with you."

"Yes, ma'am. I heard you say that. However, you can put some clothes on and come with me, or I'll cuff you and take you to the station the way you are."

"You go to hell," Cynthia said and started to close the door. Officer Carlson put his foot on the pedestal and blocked the door from closing.

"Get your foot out of the way," Cynthia told him.

"Sorry, ma'am."

Before she realized what had happened, Cynthia's back was to Carlson and he had slapped the cuffs on her. He picked her up, slung her over his shoulder, closed her front door, and carried her to the squad car. He opened the back door and gently deposited her onto the back seat.

"I'm gonna fucking kill you," she screamed.

"Yes, ma'am," he replied. "Excuse me a moment."

She watched as he went back into her house. He came out a few seconds later, carrying some clothes that she had thrown over a chair in her bedroom. He got in, started the car, and drove towards the police station.

"You are so dead," she yelled.

"Sheriff's not in a very good mood this morning."

"So, he takes it out on me?"

"He's taking it out on all of us."

A half-hour later, after putting on the clothes Officer Carlson had brought along, Cynthia was sitting on a chair across from the sheriff. His feet were up on his desk, and he was sipping a hot cup of tea. He didn't look happy.

"You look like hell," she said.

"I feel like hell," he replied.

"I'm gonna sue your ass off, you know," she said.

"I don't care. Go for it," he replied.

"You're an ass," she said.

"You should have come peacefully," he said.

"He had no right to cuff me and throw me in a car," she said.

"You shouldn't have thrown a punch. Attacking an officer of the law is a serious offense," he said.

"I did no such thing," she said.

"Sure, you did. So, you feel like answering some questions?"

"Maybe I want an attorney."

"Do you?"

"What the hell do you want, Cowboy?"

"How well did you know Sylvia Toppers?"

"I didn't know her at all. I only met her at Big John's trial."

"How's he doing, anyway?"

"Same as last time you asked me."

"What's your relationship with Steven Leyson?"

"Who?"

"Steven Leyson. He lives over on Deer Run Road."

"He's my uncle, sort of."

"What's a sort of uncle," the sheriff asked.

"He's a friend of my dad. I've always called him Uncle Steve."

"So, you're close?"

"I guess you could say that," Cynthia replied.

"You know he was dating Sylvia?" the sheriff asked.

"I heard talk."

"You didn't like her, did you?"

"I didn't know her well enough to not like her."

"You hated her because she testified against Big John, didn't you?"

"She lied. Big John never killed his mother."

"The jury found different."

"They were wrong," she said.

"You know Michael McMillan?" the sheriff asked her.

"Kind of."

"Kind of?" the sheriff said. "What's kind of knowing someone?"

"He's a friend of my aunt. I've seen him at some parties."

"Who's your aunt?"

"You know damn well who she is. You visited her yesterday."

"Rachel Hammertoe."

"What the hell do you want, Sheriff? I'm tired of this."

"Do you know a Dr. Walter White?"

"Yes."

"How well?"

"Well enough. He's done some work on my aunt."

"You still seeing Bobby Johnson?"

"No."

"Why not? What happened?" the sheriff asked.

"We parted ways, that's all. I guess I was a little too much for him."

"Really? Yeah, I can see that."

"Anything else?"

"What were you doing last Saturday night between ten and four the next morning."

"I was with Bobby. You know that."

"The entire night?"

"Yes, Sheriff, the entire night."

"Did you take a sleeping pill that night?"

"I did not."

"So, there's no way he could have slipped away for a while without you knowing it?"

"No way."

"Did he ever discuss Sylvia with you?"

"Not really. He didn't like to talk about her."

"And, you didn't know her."

"I didn't."

"Then why did you invite her to your aunt's St. Patrick's Day party?"

Cynthia simply gave the sheriff a puzzled look and said nothing.

"Well?" the sheriff inquired.

"Perhaps I need that lawyer now," Cynthia said.

"Just answer the damn question, Cynthia."

"It was because of Uncle Steve," she said. "He'd been so lonely since his wife died. We wanted to fix him up. There are not many single women his age around here, so I had my aunt invite her."

"Why lie about it, then? If that's all it was, why the big deception?"

"I guess I just didn't want to be connected with Sylvia in any way. I didn't know her that well. She was just one of a half dozen women we invited hoping he'd show some interest in one of them. Problem is, every damn man there went for her. Last I heard she had dated Uncle Steve and McMillan. I know she saw Wally, but he never mentioned what their relationship was."

"Wally? You mean Dr. White?" the sheriff asked.

"Yes, Dr. White. I mean, how many men did she need, for crying out loud? I'm not even sure if she ever quit seeing Bobby. He said they only dated a little while, but I think he still had the hots for her."

"You know Dr. White is in the hospital in serious condition? Do you know why he was leaving town?"

"Why don't you ask him?"

"It seems he's slipped into a coma. What can you tell me about him?"

"Nice enough person, I guess. He's a great plastic surgeon. Just look at how great my aunt looks. He's done a lot of work on her."

"I noticed," said the sheriff, trying not to smile.

"His mother lives in Florida. Perhaps, he was going to visit her."

"Well, if he was, it was a last-minute thing. His receptionist had to cancel all his appointments for the next two weeks."

"I wouldn't know about that."

"How's Big John's appeal coming?"

"Not good. It's too bad Sylvia's gone. She was probably the only person who could have helped. If we could just have gotten her to tell the truth," Cynthia said.

"We? Who's we?"

"I mean – I don't know who. You, maybe. Or, Big John's attorney. Someone."

"Maybe you and someone tried to persuade her to change her story. Maybe it got out of hand. Is that what happened, Cynthia? Did you and one of your friends take it a little too far?"

"I don't know what the hell you're talking about. It seems to me that you're reaching."

"You had a phone call late Saturday night. Who was it?"

"A wrong number."

"You sure about that?"

"Positive."

The sheriff stared at her for a few seconds. He took his feet off the desk and stretched.

"Think I'm ready for a cup of coffee. This tea isn't doing the job. You want one?"

"I just want to leave. Are we done here?"

"Tim," the sheriff yelled. "Get in here."

Tim walked into the room, smiling. "Yes, Sir."

"Would you please give Ms. Hughes a ride home? We're done for now."

"Be glad to," he replied.

"I'm not getting in a car with that Neanderthal," she said.

"It's him, a cab, or you walk," said the sheriff.

"Call me a cab," she replied.

As she walked out of the station to get into a cab, the sheriff smiled. That's a whole lot of woman, he thought, and a bloody liar.

"Casey," he yelled. "It's safe for you to come in here now. She's gone."

Friday Morning

"Did you visit Myrtle this morning?"

"Yes, I did, and I took her donuts."

"Did she remember anything?"

"She did. She told me she saw a car pull up around midnight, a man got out, and he threw a body into the lake. He was about 5'10" tall with brown hair and blue eyes. He had a tattoo on his shoulder that looked like an eagle," Funtelli told the sheriff.

The sheriff stared at him. "Okay, you made your point. You don't need to keep taking her donuts. She doesn't know anything."

"Thank you," Funtelli said.

"We finished searching White's house and office," Casey told the sheriff.

"Find anything?" the sheriff inquired.

"We went through the files on his computer. It seems he took a lot of pictures of his patients, but mostly for medical reasons. The pictures of Sylvia were not ordinary. As far as we can tell, he only took full nude shots of her and two other women," Casey told him.

"Who are the other two?"

"Caroline Simpson and Cynthia Hughes," said Casey.

"Who's Simpson?" the sheriff asked.

"No idea. We're checking her out. All we know right now is that she has one hot body. I'd say the best of the three. She is really gorgeous. I'm telling you, Sheriff, I'd give. . . "

"You been getting any, Casey?" the sheriff interrupted.

"Sorry. Having a baby is stressful in more ways than one."

Sheriff Berkson laughed. "Give it a little time, Casey. Things eventually get back to normal."

"Anyway," Casey said, "We're checking her out. They didn't find much at White's house. No gun there. Forensics is running a DNA test to see if his semen matches," Casey told the sheriff.

"No sign that Sylvia had been there?"

"None. We did find plastic bags in his house, like the one that robe was tied up in. They're a popular brand, though. We brought in a few open wine bottles that were in his fridge. We're hoping they might be a match to what Sylvia had in her stomach. That's reaching, though. She swallowed a lot of water, so it diluted the stomach contents."

"White has a pool, right?" the sheriff asked Casey.

"Yeah. Why?"

"Let's see when the last time his filter was changed. I want a sample of his pool water. Tell Tim to get over there and get one. If it's even close, we're gonna filter that water."

"You got a feeling about this, Sheriff?" Funtelli asked.

"I got a feeling."

"Sheriff, I have something," Officer Herzberg said, looking up from his computer.

"Whataya got, Brad?" the sheriff asked.

"Caroline Simpson is dead. She died about eighteen months ago under suspicious circumstances."

"What was her cause of death?"

"She drowned in Walter White's pool. There are some crime scene photos. God, she was beautiful, even in death. It says here that she was a model in New York. Her family lives in Branson and she'd been here visiting."

"So, what was her connection with White?"

"It only says that she attended a party at White's house. White found her in the morning, floating in his pool. He told police that she had asked to sleep on his couch, as she had drunk a lot and didn't want to drive home. Other guests who attended the party agreed that she had been drinking heavily. After an extensive investigation, it was ruled an accidental drowning."

"We need to get forensics over to White's house," the sheriff said. "I want every inch of his house examined. It's been almost a week and I'm sure the house has been cleaned, so check his vacuum bags. Luminol the floors and walls for blood. Don't miss a fucking inch of his house, understand? I think he's our guy and I want to nail that bastard."

153

"On it," said Brad.

"Casey, get me Doc Harris on the phone. He's the county coroner. Let's see what he can tell us about the Simpson drowning. We better talk to Cynthia again. If she wasn't a patient, then why the hell did she pose naked for White? Did those two have something going on?"

Steve Leyson had not slept for almost a week. He knew he was going to be caught. He hadn't lied when he said Sylvia wasn't at his house on Saturday, but he hadn't exactly told the truth. He had seen her, just not at his house.

It was only a matter of time before they matched his DNA to the semen that they had to have found in her body. Then, he would be suspected of killing her. He had no solid alibi. He was going to be convicted of her murder. He just knew it.

Michael McMillan was leaving town. He'd had enough crap from Sheriff Berkson. There was no doubt in McMillan's mind that the sheriff was trying to pin Sylvia's murder on him. The very fact that he couldn't account for two of the robes was enough to make the sheriff suspicious. He had business in Chicago, and this was as good a time as any to take a trip.

He pulled his suitcase down from a shelf in his bedroom, opened it, and started throwing clothes in. As he reached under his bed for his slippers, something sparkly inside the left slipper caught his eye. He tipped it over and a silver earring fell out. He picked it up and smiled. It was Sylvia's. She had looked high and low for it a few weeks ago after they had made love. Now, he held a part of her in his hand.

Bobby Johnson shook the bank manager's hand. He had called Bobby to let him know that Big John's house had just gone into foreclosure. Bobby decided the right thing to do would be to buy the house. Even though Cynthia was still living there, she had never made a payment on the mortgage. The likelihood of Big John ever living there again was slim, but Bobby wanted to keep the house for him, just in case.

It's the least I can do, he thought. After all, he is doing my time. And, I did screw his girlfriend, even if it was her idea. Tom will be out of prison in a few years. It could be a place for him to live when he gets out.

I'm not sure what I'll do about Cynthia, he thought. I can't wait to see the look on her face when I tell her she's living in my house and she needs to start paying rent. She will be pissed.

He felt good about what he had just done. Yes, sir, he thought, I sure am a good brother.

Friday Morning - Two

"We have a match," Casey told the sheriff. "Steve Leyson."

"Not White? I figured it would be White," the sheriff said.

"Nope. Looks like the last guy she had sex with was Leyson. He told us he didn't see her on Saturday."

"Go bring him in. I'll get a search warrant for his house."

He knew he was in trouble when he heard the knock on the door, looked out the window, and saw the squad car parked in front of his house. He took a deep breath, let it out, and answered the door.

"Hey, Deputy. What can I do for you this morning?"

"Sheriff wants to talk to you."

"What about?"

"Let's go."

"Can you at least tell me what this is all about?"

"No, Leyson, I can't. You coming peacefully or do I have to cuff you?"

"Take it easy, Casey. I'm coming."

Sheriff Berkson watched Casey and Leyson as they walked into the police station. Leyson looked about as guilty as a kid who was caught with his hand in the cookie jar.

"Morning, Sheriff," Leyson said.

"Morning. It seems we have a problem, Mr. Leyson."

"Call me Steve. No sense being all formal."

"Well, Steve, we have a big problem."

"What would that be, Sheriff?"

"You lied to us, Steve. You said you didn't see Sylvia on Saturday."

"Actually, Sheriff," Leyson said, "I think I said she didn't come over to my house on Saturday. I never said I didn't see her."

"You like playing fucking games, Steve? Your DNA matches the semen found in her body. You had sex with her on Saturday night before you killed her."

"I didn't kill her."

"Unless you can give me one hell of an alibi, I'm arresting you for her murder."

"I didn't do it. Okay, I saw her on Saturday. But it was only for a few minutes. I dropped a check off at her house, and well – we had a quickie – okay?"

"What time was that?"

"Around six or six-thirty. I wanted to stay, but she said she had a party she was going to and had to get ready."

"What was the check for?"

"She was still doing some work for me and I owed her. I gave her the check on Friday night, but she forgot it. I drove over and gave it to her on Saturday. That's all. That's the last time I saw her."

"Did she tell you whose party it was?"

"I didn't ask and she didn't tell. Even if I had, she wouldn't have told me. Sylvia didn't share personal stuff. I have no idea whose party it was."

"You're a liar, Steve. Tell me why I should believe you now. What else aren't you telling me?"

"Nothing. I swear, Sheriff, that's it. I would never have hurt her."

"Here's what I'm gonna do, Steve. I'm gonna lock you up for a while. Then, my men are gonna go search your house. They're probably going to find the gun that killed her. Then, I'm gonna arrest you for her murder."

"I didn't kill her."

"We'll see, Steve. In the meantime, while you're locked up, you should spend some time praying we don't find that gun. Or, you could just confess now and get it over with."

"I'm sorry I lied to you, Sheriff, but I didn't do it. You're wasting your time searching my house. You aren't gonna find anything there."

"Lock him up, Casey."

"Do you remember seeing a check from Leyson when we searched Sylvia's house?" the sheriff asked Casey, after he returned from locking up Leyson.

"I don't. It could be in with her papers. We gave most of those to her sister, though. Let me ask Brad if he remembers seeing a check."

Brad looked up from his computer. "You talking about me?" he inquired.

"Do you remember seeing a check, to Sylvia from Leyson, in with all those papers we brought back from her house?" Casey asked him.

"Sure do. There was a check from him and another one from Michael McMillan."

"Good god," said the sheriff. "It just gets better. How much was the check for?"

"Let me check the list."

"Well?" said the sheriff.

"Just a second," answered Brad, as he pulled up the inventory of items removed from Sylvia's house.

"Leyson gave her a check for $675.00. The notation on the check said, 'Computer Services'.

"What's the one from McMillan?"

"McMillan gave her a check for $800.00. That notation said, 'love you, hope this helps'.

"Hope this helps for what?" the sheriff asked.

"No idea," replied Brad. "Anything else you need?"

"What are the dates of the checks?"

"Leyson's was last Friday. The check from McMillan was dated three weeks ago."

"I wonder why she didn't cash it," commented the sheriff. "Brad, have Funtelli go pick up that warrant for Leyson's house. I want him and Tim to get over there and tear that place apart. I want that gun."

"Casey, you're with me," said the sheriff, as he headed towards the door.

"Where we going?" Casey asked.

"McMillan's."

Nurse Caroline stood at the end of Dr. White's hospital bed, staring at her patient. It was time to push the button again and she didn't want to do it. She wanted him to suffer. In fact, she wanted the pig dead.

She glanced towards the door to make sure no one was looking. Then, she gently pulled the needle out of the back of his hand and pushed the button, which released the morphine. She let the solution drip into the puke pan for a few seconds and then replaced the needle. She emptied the pan into the sink in the bathroom and washed it down the drain.

She checked his vitals and recorded them in his patient log, making sure she noted that he had received his pain medication. She smiled and walked out of his room.

<u>Friday Noon</u>

McMillan threw his suitcase into the backseat of his car, got in, and started the engine. He swore, turned off the key, and ran back into the house. He grabbed his laptop and cell phone off the counter and looked around the house. Okay to go, he thought and headed back out to his car.

He stopped dead in his tracks when he saw the squad car sitting in front of his garage.

"You going somewhere, McMillan?" the sheriff asked.

"I've got a business meeting in Chicago and I'm already getting a late start. What could you possibly want now?"

"You gave Sylvia a check for $850.00 a few weeks ago. What was that for?"

"The check was for $800.00, not $850.00. She lost one of her earrings in my house and we couldn't find it. The money was a gift. I wanted her to replace them."

"Pretty expensive earrings," commented Casey.

"Anything else? I've got to get going," said McMillan.

"You have a couple of choices, here," said the sheriff. "You either stay in town voluntarily or I make you a guest at my jail until this case is solved. You're still a suspect and I want you here."

"Sheriff, how many times do I have to tell you? I had nothing to do with Sylvia's death. I've got a business to run and

I've got a client waiting in Chicago. This is downright harassment."

"Call it whatever you want. You're staying in town. I guess I can put a leg monitor on you to make sure you stay around. Be better than having to feed you at the jail."

"You have nothing on me and you know it. You know what, Sheriff? I want you to arrest me, right now. Then, I'll call my lawyer and I'll file charges against you and your crazy ass way of doing things."

"You gonna stay in town?"

"You going to solve this case pretty soon?"

"I'm working on it," the sheriff replied.

"Alright. You quit harassing me and I'll stick around for a few more days. But I'll tell you right now, on Monday morning I'm heading out to meet with my client in Chicago. Deal?"

"I'll go along with that, McMillan. Unless we find something between now and Monday morning that lands you in jail."

Sheriff Berkson and Casey drove off, leaving a frustrated McMillan standing in the driveway of his home.

"He sure seems guilty to me," said Casey.

"I kinda like him for it, too," replied the sheriff. "To be honest with you, I don't know who to believe and who not to believe. All three seem guilty to me."

"That your phone ringing?" asked Casey.

Sheriff Berkson answered his phone, said a few ah huhs, and hung up.

"That was Brad. White came out of his coma," he told Casey.

"We going over there?"

"Sure are. Right after we stop for some hot coffee."

"He's awake. You can go in, but only for a few minutes. I don't want you to upset him," Dr. Wasserstein told the sheriff.

"How's he doing?"

"He's in a lot of pain. He keeps asking for more pain medication. I don't understand it. We've got him on morphine, so the pain should be minimal."

"So, he's gonna pull through?"

"He should. We've removed his spleen, which was ruptured. His ribs will heal. There's still some internal bleeding, which isn't good. We put his hand back together the best we could, but he'll never be able to hold a scalpel again."

"Thanks, Doc. I'm only gonna ask him a few questions and we'll leave."

"Just don't upset him."

Dr. Walter White couldn't stop moaning. He was in horrible pain and he wasn't scheduled to get more morphine for a couple of hours.

Sheriff Berkson and Casey stood in the doorway, looking at him. There was hardly a part of his exposed body that wasn't bruised. It made them wonder what the rest of his body must look like.

"How you doing, Dr. White?" the sheriff asked.

White stopped his moaning and looked over at the two men. "Get out. I don't want to talk to you," he uttered, in a weak voice.

"Casey," said the sheriff, "Shut the door."

"Got it," said Casey.

"That was some kind of accident," said the sheriff. "You should see your car. I can't believe you weren't killed. You are one lucky man, Doc."

"What do you want, Sheriff? Can't you see I'm in pain?"

"You look like you are. You look terrible. In fact, you look so bad, you probably look worse than most dead people."

"You here to aggravate me, Sheriff?"

"Not at all. You want I should push that morphine button that you can't reach?"

"God, yes. Oh, would you? Please. I don't know how much longer I can stand this pain."

"I'll be happy to. Just as soon as you answer a few questions for me."

"Anything. What do you want to know?"

"Well, first off, Doc, I want to know if you were having an affair with Cynthia Hughes."

"Of course not. I only know Cynthia through her aunt. We're just acquaintances."

"Then how come you have all those naked pictures of her?"

"You looked at my computer? You can't do that. Those are private."

"Sure I can and I did. So, why the naked pictures?"

"If I tell you, will you push that button?"

"Sure will."

"She wanted a favor. I told her I'd do it if she posed naked for me. She didn't mind. I think she enjoyed posing like that. She likes to show off those breasts of hers."

"She sure does," Casey injected into the conversation.

"What was the favor she wanted?" the sheriff asked, ignoring Casey's remark.

"I can't remember. It was a while back," said White.

"How long ago?" asked the sheriff.

"Please. You promised. Push the button."

"In a minute. What was the favor?"

"She wanted me to get close to Sylvia Toppers and see if I could find out anything about Melissa Johnson's murder. Now, for god's sake, push that button."

"Did you?"

"Did I what?"

"Get close to Sylvia," said the sheriff.

"I tried, but she wouldn't date me. She wasn't interested."

The door to White's room opened and Dr. Wasserstein stuck his head in.

"I think you've bothered my patient long enough, Sheriff. Time to go."

White, obviously in pain, looked at the doctor and said, "I'm fine. They can stay a few more minutes. We aren't quite done here, are we, Sheriff?"

"Just a couple more questions and we'll be out of here, Doc," Sheriff Berkson replied.

"Three more minutes. That's it, okay?" Doctor Wasserstein said.

"Right," said the sheriff. "Three minutes."

As the doctor closed the door, White said, "Okay, Sheriff, push that button. I answered your damn questions."

"One more," said the sheriff, as he walked over to the side of White's bed and placed his finger on the button. "Did you kill Sylvia Toppers?"

"No," said White, almost sobbing now.

"Wrong answer," said the sheriff. He turned and started to walk out of the room.

"Wait," yelled White. "I didn't want to do it, but she made me."

"She made you kill her? Just how does that happen, Doc? How does somebody make you kill them?" asked the sheriff.

"It just went too far. I didn't mean to do it. It was an accident. Please, I can't stand the pain anymore."

"So, you're telling me that you almost drowned her, choked her, then shot her, and it was all an accident. That's one hell of an accident, Doc."

"Yes. Now push that goddamn button, will you?"

"Doctor White, you are confessing to killing Sylvia Toppers?"

"Yes. I did it, okay?" White answered

"You got that, Casey?"

"Sure do, Sheriff. Recorded every last word."

"Read him his rights. I don't think he'll be going anywhere, but secure him to the bed, just in case he decides to take another trip."

"Are you gonna push that button now?" Doctor White asked, as tears ran down his cheeks.

"Sorry, Doctor, you know I'm not allowed to do that. Let me get your nurse. Caroline, isn't it? Maybe, she'll be able to help you out."

Friday Afternoon

In a small town like Hollister, it didn't take long for news to spread. By noon, half the population knew that Dr. White had been arrested for Sylvia's murder.

During his lunch at Minnie's Diner, almost every customer congratulated Sheriff Berkson on a job well done. By the time he walked back to his office, he was feeling pretty darn proud of himself.

When he walked through the office door, he noticed a woman talking to Casey. A woman he definitely did not want to talk to. He turned to leave, hoping she hadn't seen him, but he was too late.

"You going somewhere, Sheriff?"

Sheriff Berkson turned back towards the room and forced a smile. "Good afternoon, Ms. Murphy."

"Maybe it's a good afternoon for you, Sheriff. It certainly is not for my client."

"And, who would that client be?"

"You know damned well who it is. I've just had a long talk with Walter White. He may be in pain, but he certainly remembers what happened in his room a few hours ago. He would have confessed to the Lindbergh baby kidnapping to get some relief. You coerced him into that confession and I'll have it thrown out faster than a speeding bullet. What the hell is wrong with you? Are you so anxious to close a case that you'll torture a person to get a confession? I'll have your fucking badge, by the time I'm done with you."

"He's guilty."

"He says otherwise."

"We have his taped confession, Francine. It'll stand up in court."

"You promised him morphine if he confessed that he killed Sylvia. You actually think a judge is going to allow that?"

"He's guilty."

"This case isn't closed, Cowboy. You have a coerced confession. That's all you've got. Where's the gun? What's the motive? Where's your evidence? You've got nothing."

"The arrest stands."

"Not for long, it doesn't," she said, as she started to leave. "You should be ashamed of yourself."

Casey watched her leave, and then asked, "Could we have made a mistake, Sheriff?"

"We didn't make a mistake, Casey. We got the man. Now we just have to get the evidence."

Cynthia Hughes opened the door and asked Bobby to come in. It was a little after twelve noon, and she was still wearing her nightie.

"You miss me, Bobby?"

"Not really. We have business to discuss. You want to put some clothes on?"

"No, I'm fine just like this."

"Then at least cover up."

"Seriously? I thought you enjoyed looking at my body."

"Not today, Cynthia."

"So, what's this business we have to discuss? You look so serious," she said teasingly. Suddenly, a look of real concern came over her face, and she asked, "Did something happen to Big John? Is he okay?"

"He's fine. It's about you living here."

"What about it?"

"After Big John went to jail, you didn't make even one mortgage payment. The house went into foreclosure, so I bought it."

"Well, good for you. But, what has that got to do with me?"

"Well, Cynthia, what it has to do with you, is that you are no longer going to live here rent-free."

"You expect me to pay you rent? I don't think so. You owe me."

"I owe you? Why in the world do I owe you?" Bobby asked.

"Because I know you killed your mother and I've kept my mouth shut. Big John's doing your time, Bobby, and you know it. I'd be living here with him now if it wasn't for you. You at least owe me a place to live."

"Wow," Bobby exclaimed. "I guess you do think I killed my mom. You are so far off base. I want you out of here. Today, Cynthia. I don't want to see you or talk to you again. Pack up your shit and get out. If you don't, I'll have the sheriff evict you."

"You're a bastard. You know that, Bobby. You're a murderer and a bastard. Get out of here."

"I may be a bastard, but I'm sure as hell not a murderer – yet. You are tempting me, though. And, for your information, I'm not going anywhere. You go get dressed, get your crap together, and get out. You've got fifteen minutes and then, if you're not gone, I'm gonna throw your sorry ass out of here."

"Fuck you, Bobby," she screamed.

"You already did. Now get out of my house."

"You miss her, Bobby?" Cynthia said, her voice barely a whisper.

"Miss who?" Bobby asked.

"Sylvia, of course. Do you miss her? I know you loved her. Every man she met loved her. How did that make you feel, Bobby? Knowing that she was screwing all those men. Did it make you angry? Perhaps, it made you so angry you killed her. Did you kill her Bobby, just like you killed your mother?

"Shut your mouth, Cynthia."

"What's the matter, Bobby? Does the truth hurt?"

"Where are your car keys?"

"What do you want my keys for?"

Bobby walked into the kitchen and looked around. He saw the keys on the counter, picked them up, and removed the house keys. He went back into the living room, threw the remaining keys at her, and opened the front door.

"Get out," he said, threatening.

"Bobby, please," she begged. "I'm sorry. I didn't mean it."

Bobby walked over to her, grabbed her arm, and walked her to the door.

"Bye, Cynthia," he said, shoved her out of the house, and closed the door.

Fifteen minutes later, Cynthia Hughes walked through the door to the police station. Casey glanced over at the sheriff and said, "Holy crap."

"Casey, I want you out of here," the sheriff said.

"But, Sheriff . . . "

"Get in the backroom and stay there," the sheriff interrupted.

"Brad," the sheriff said. "Get me a jacket."

"Why?" Brad asked the sheriff.

"Why the hell do you think?" the sheriff replied. "Go get a jacket, so we can cover Cynthia up."

"Okay," said Brad, still sitting in his chair, staring at Cynthia.

"Funtelli," the sheriff yelled.

Officer Funtelli walked out of a backroom, carrying a jacket, and handed it to the sheriff.

"Thank you," said the sheriff.

Cynthia stood in the middle of the police station, in her revealing short, thin nightie, obviously enjoying the chaos she was causing.

"Sheriff Berkson, I would like you to arrest Bobby Johnson."

The sheriff walked over to Cynthia and handed her the jacket. "Please put this on. And, zip it up."

Cynthia smiled, as she took the jacket and put it on, leaving the front open.

"Zip it up," the sheriff said.

"Fine," she said and zipped up the jacket.

"Why do you want me to arrest Bobby?" the sheriff asked.

"He threw me out of my house. He came barging in and told me to get out. He didn't even let me get dressed, as you can see. All my things are in that house. I want him arrested."

"Take a chair. Wait. Funtelli, put something on that chair for Ms. Hughes to sit on. I believe that wood might be a little chilly for her bare behind," said the sheriff.

"She might stick to it, too," said Funtelli, with a smirk.

"Get a pillow or something, and no more comments."

After the sheriff made sure that Cynthia was comfortable, he sat down behind his desk and studied her. She is beautiful, he thought, and dangerous. If Bobby tossed her out, he had a reason.

"Tell me what happened. It doesn't sound like something Bobby would do without a reason."

"I might have made him mad. But, that's still no reason to throw me out."

"How did you make him mad?"

"I might have accused him of killing his mother. But I said it in anger."

"Cynthia, I want you to stay right here for a minute. I'll be right back."

Sheriff Berkson left his desk and walked into a room in the back of the jail. Casey was drinking a cup of coffee while pretending to be studying a wanted poster.

"Get Bobby Johnson down here right now. I want to know why Cynthia walked in here half-naked."

"You want me to go get him or call him?" Casey asked.

"He might still be at Cynthia's house. Drive over there and bring him back here."

"I'm on it."

Fifteen minutes later, Casey and Bobby Johnson walked into the police station. Casey was carrying a large box, overflowing with clothes.

"Get him away from me," Cynthia yelled.

"He's not anywhere near you," the sheriff told her. "You just settle down."

"What's the story, Casey?" the sheriff asked.

"Bobby owns the house. He bought it when the bank foreclosed on it. It's his, free and clear. He was gonna let her stay there and pay rent, but she said she wouldn't, so he told her to get out."

"That true, Bobby?" the sheriff asked.

"Mostly. I also gave her a chance to get dressed, but she refused. Casey has most of her clothes in that box. She can pick up the rest later if someone from your office is with her. She's got a nasty mouth on her, Sheriff, and I don't want her telling tales that aren't true."

"That true, Cynthia? Did Bobby give you a chance to get dressed?"

"Not really," she answered.

"Did he tell you that you could stay there if you paid rent?"

"Kinda," she replied.

"Then, I find that Bobby had every right to ask you to leave. Get some clothes out of that box that Casey set down over there, and get dressed. Let me know when you want to pick up the rest of your things and I'll have an officer accompany you."

"You aren't gonna arrest Bobby?"

"No."

"He killed his mother, you know."

"Well, Big John was convicted for that crime. It's a closed case."

"Well, maybe you should open it, Sheriff."

"By the way, Cynthia, how well do you know Dr. White?"

"I thought I already told you. He's my aunt's doctor."

"Did you ever see him professionally?"

"Do I look like I need work done?"

"You certainly do not," answered the sheriff. "If you weren't a patient, why does he have all those nude photos of you?"

"Have you seen them?" she asked the sheriff. "How are they?"

"They're just fine. You haven't seen them?"

"No, he wouldn't show me."

"How come you posed for those pictures, Cynthia?"

"He asked me to."

"For what reason?"

"I guess I owed him. It was no big deal. They're just pictures."

"Why'd you owe him?"

"He did me a favor."

"What favor?"

"Nothing important, Sheriff. I barely remember what it was."

"Perhaps, you wanted him to get close to Sylvia so he could pump her for information."

"Perhaps, I did. I needed her to tell the truth, so Big John could get his appeal."

"What makes you so sure she didn't tell the truth?"

"Because Big John is innocent, we know it wasn't Tom, and that leaves Bobby."

"That's quite a leap. Even if Big John is innocent, it could be anyone else. You don't know it was Bobby."

"I just know."

Friday Afternoon - Two

"Francine Murphy got the judge to throw out the arrest."

"On what grounds? He confessed," said Casey.

"He says the confession was coerced," Sheriff Berkson said. "Judge Peterson says I need a lot more evidence, than what we've got before we can arrest him again."

"We did kinda force him into saying he did it," Casey commented. "Man, he was really suffering."

"He really was. It was like he hadn't been given anything for his pain at all. I guess we did take advantage of the situation. By the way, have the results of his pool water come in yet?"

"No. I'll give the lab a call and see what the holdup is," Casey said.

"Do that and let me know," the sheriff told him.

"You've got that look. Whatcha thinking?" Casey asked him.

"When he was at her place last Saturday, Sylvia told Leyson that she had to get ready for a party she was going to. I need to find out who held that party."

"We know it wasn't Rachel Hammertoe. She didn't have a party last Saturday night. It would have been in that book."

"I'm running on fumes here, Casey. We know Leyson was the last person to have sex with her, but there's no evidence against him. McMillan was upset because she turned down his marriage proposal and he's got one hell of a temper. He's missing two white robes, which is suspicious, but not enough to arrest him. Also, he was trying to leave town. It seems White was obsessed with her, taking those nude pictures when it wasn't necessary. Also, Cynthia was trying to get him to pump Sylvia for information about Bobby and his mother's murder."

"Then there's that damn party," said Casey. "You know, Sheriff, Rachel Hammertoe knows everything that goes on in this town. Even if she didn't throw the party, perhaps she knows who did. I think we should talk to her again."

"It can't hurt. Let's drive over there and see if she's home. I'm sick of being as stumped as a one-legged pirate."

"I'm sorry, Sheriff. I can't help you. I don't know of any parties that were held last Saturday night."

"Think hard, Mrs. Hammertoe," the sheriff said. "Do you remember anyone mentioning a party? It doesn't have to be a big formal party. Maybe just a last-minute get-together. Perhaps, Cynthia mentioned something to you."

"I don't talk to her that often, you know. Did you know that horrible man kicked her out of her house? That poor girl is going to have to move back home and live with her parents. At least, until she can get back on her feet."

"Who did you hear that from? It just happened a few hours ago," the sheriff inquired.

"Well, her mother is my sister, you know. We talk a couple of times a day. We're very close. She told me."

"Do you remember if Cynthia's mother mentioned anything to you about a party or a get-together?"

"I don't believe so. However . . . "

"What?" the sheriff asked.

"Well, it probably doesn't mean anything. I just remembered that Wally – I mean, Dr. White – mentioned he was having a few people over on Saturday. Kind of a last-minute thing. But Cynthia wasn't invited. Her mother would have told me. So, it probably doesn't mean anything."

"When did you talk to Dr. White?"

"It was on Thursday. I had an appointment with him. Isn't it sad what happened to him? I hear he's in such bad shape. I hope he'll be okay."

"I'm sure he'll be just fine. Did he mention who he had asked to his little get-together?"

"Well, no names. He did say he had invited a couple of people he had met at my St. Patrick's Day party. He said he wanted to get to know them better. That could be anyone, though. There were over a hundred people at that party."

A little way down the road from the Hammertoe's house, Sheriff Berkson pulled the car over to the side of the road and stopped. Casey looked at him, wondering what was going on in that head of his, now.

"We're going back to the hospital, aren't we?" Casey asked.

"I'm gonna see if White will tell us who was at that party. I think that's the key to this whole thing."

"You gonna get that?" Casey asked. "You're phone's ringing."

The sheriff listened for a few seconds to the voice on the other end of the call. He looked over at Casey, obviously not happy about the call.

"Who was that?" Casey asked.

"Brad. He got the test results of the water from White's pool. He's had his pool winterized, so the lab couldn't get a match."

"Already? It seems kind of early for that. Well, the water's a dead end, then. We only know for sure that the water in Sylvia's lungs didn't come from Leyson. McMillan and White are both maybes."

"Let's see what White has to say," the sheriff said.

"Do you really think he's gonna talk to us, after what we put him through?" Casey asked.

"We can only hope," said the sheriff.

Friday Afternoon - Three

"You can't go in there," Doctor Wasserstein told the sheriff. "You've caused enough trouble."

"I'm sorry about that, Doc. I guess I got a little carried away."

"You think? You promised him morphine, for crying out loud."

"I just have one question. You come in with us. If you think it's too much for him, I'll leave. This is important."

"I don't know, Cowboy. That lawyer lady may have my ass if I let you in there again. I don't want to do anything to cause this hospital to get into trouble."

"One question. Please, Doc."

"I just know I'm gonna hate myself for this. Alright, but I'm coming in the room with you."

"Thanks, Doc. How's he doing this morning?"

"Better."

Doctor White was sleeping. He was getting regulated doses of his pain medication and it made him tired. Voices filtered through to his sleeping brain and he slowly opened his eyes. He smiled when he saw Doctor Wasserstein standing by his bed.

"Morning, Philip," he mumbled.

"Morning, Walter. The sheriff is here to apologize to you for this morning. He feels really bad. I don't want you to get upset, and if you don't want to talk to him, I'll ask him to leave."

"If he's afraid I'm going to sue his ass, he's right. He can apologize until the cows come home; it won't make any difference."

White glanced towards the door and saw Sheriff Berkson standing there. "Come on in, Sheriff. Philip tells me you have something you want to say to me. What would that be?"

Sheriff Berkson approached his bed, head down, hat in hand. "I just want to say I'm sorry. What I did was mean and I know you only confessed because you were in pain."

"Damned right it was mean. You arrested me and had me tied to my bed. I'm a doctor, for god's sake. I don't hurt people, I help them."

"Yes, Sir, and I'm sorry."

"You're not supposed to be here you know."

"I know, but I was hoping you could answer just one more question for me."

"Philip, what the hell is going on? You let him in here with the pretense he's apologizing and now he's going to question me again?"

"Not at all, Walter. He's sincere about that apology. He did mention he had one question to ask you. I don't see how that could hurt if it helps find out who murdered Sylvia."

"One question and that's it. Alright, Sheriff, ask your one question and then get the hell out of here."

"Who did you invite to your party last Saturday night?"

"I didn't have a party. I had a few friends over. There's a big difference between having a party and just entertaining a few friends, you know."

"Yes, Sir, I guess there is. Sorry. A bad choice of words. So, could you tell me who was there?"

"I don't know if I should. You'll probably arrest me again, for lying."

"I'm not gonna arrest you for lying. I promise."

"Well, Cynthia Hughes was there. She was one of the guests, but she left right after we ate. She said she had to meet someone."

"Who else?"

"Sylvia Toppers was there."

"Is that all?"

"Michael McMillan. I don't know if you know him. He and Sylvia left together. Well, not exactly together. They left at the same time. They both had their own cars there."

"So, there were just the four of you for dinner?"

"That's right. The four of us."

"Thank you, Doctor White. I appreciate your help."

"Fine. Now, please leave."

The sheriff started to walk out of the room, turned, and said, "Just one more thing, Doctor. You mentioned that Cynthia had asked you to get close to Sylvia, so you could pump her for information about Bobby and his mother's death. Did you ever find out anything?"

"I told you before, we didn't get that close. I brought it up once, and Sylvia made it very clear that she wouldn't discuss it. So, I guess the answer is no. I didn't find out anything, Sheriff."

"Sorry, I bothered you. Thanks, again," the sheriff said.

"Why do you figure he lied to us when we questioned him the first time?" Casey asked the sheriff, as they left the hospital. "So, what if he had company? Why the big cover-up?"

"What's even more interesting is why McMillan lied about being home all night," the sheriff replied.

"You still think White did it?" Casey asked.

"I'm having some doubts. I would have sworn it was him."

"So, that means that it was probably Leyson or McMillan," Casey commented.

"Call Funtelli. Tell him to bring McMillan in. Let's sweat him a little and see what we can find out."

Officer Funtelli met Sheriff Berkson and his deputy, as they walked into the police station. "He's in Room One, and he's madder than a wet hen," Funtelli told the sheriff.

"Tough. What did you tell him?"

"Just that you had some questions. He started to resist, but thought better about it."

The sheriff laughed. "I'd think better about it, too, before I'd try to take you on. Go ask him if he wants something to drink. He's gonna be here for a while."

"Already did. He didn't want anything."

"Go ask him again," the sheriff said.

Sheriff Berkson waited another fifteen minutes before he went in to see McMillan. As soon as the sheriff walked in, McMillan jumped out of his chair and started to approach him.

"Sit," said the sheriff.

"Just what the hell do you think you're doing? Do you think you can drag me down here, like a common criminal? This harassment has gone far enough, Sheriff. I want my attorney and I want him now."

"Why would you want an attorney? I haven't arrested you for anything. I just want to ask you a couple of questions. Then, I'll probably arrest you and, then, you can call your attorney."

"You're not funny," McMillan yelled. "I'm going home."

"No, you're not. What you are going to do is sit your ass down in that chair and answer every question I ask you, and answer them honestly. If I catch you in one more lie, I will arrest you for impeding a murder investigation. Is that clear? Now, sit your ass down."

"You are going to be so sorry," McMillan muttered, as he sat back down.

"Won't be the first time," the sheriff said. "Now, Mr. McMillan, I will be recording this. So, just make sure you tell the truth."

"Whatever," McMillan said, under his breath.

"Where were you last Saturday night?"

"I already told you. I was home. Alone."

"Lie number one. You want to try that again?"

"I was home. That's the truth."

"Let's start again. Where were you last Saturday night between seven and ten?"

"I was home. That's where I was and that story is not going to change."

"So, you weren't having dinner at Doctor White's home?"

"Why in the world would I be having dinner at his house? I don't even know the man."

"You know him. You met him at a party at Rachel Hammertoe's. A St. Patrick's Day party. You met both him and Sylvia there."

"Yes, I met Sylvia at that party. I don't remember a Doctor White, though."

"Well, he sure remembers you. He remembers you so well that he invited you to his house last Saturday for dinner."

"He did what?" McMillan asked, laughing. "You have got to be fucking kidding me. If he told you that story and you believed it, then you're both crazy. I was nowhere near his house last Saturday."

"How well do you know Cynthia Hughes?"

"Cynthia? I know her, but not real well. Her aunt is Rachel Hammertoe. I know her through her aunt."

"Was she at White's dinner on Saturday?"

"How the hell should I know," McMillan yelled. "I wasn't fucking there."

An hour later, an exasperated Sheriff Berkson left the interrogation room. He poured himself a cup of coffee, took a swallow, and made a disgusted face. "For crying out loud, Casey, can't someone around here make a decent cup of coffee?"

"Sorry, Sheriff. That's been sitting there a while. I'll make a fresh pot."

"Forget it. Get me a Coke. With caffeine. I need caffeine."

"You get anywhere with him?" Casey asked.

"He's sticking to his story. He was home. He says he knows Cynthia, but not White. I'm beginning to think he's telling the truth."

"Then, that means that White fed you a story about having him over for dinner."

"I want to talk to Cynthia. Where would she be this time of day?"

"How should I know?"

"Get Funtelli to find her," said the sheriff. "I'm going back in."

While McMillan was still being questioned by the sheriff, Cynthia Hughes was being escorted into the police station by Officer Funtelli.

"I'm getting real tired of this crap," she told Funtelli, as he helped her out of the squad car. "What does that idiot sheriff of yours want now?"

"I have no idea, ma'am."

"Ma'am? Do I look like a ma'am to you?"

"Yes ma'am. Watch your step, please."

"You are so polite, it's disgusting," Cynthia said.

"Yes, ma'am."

191

"Put her in Room Two," Casey told Funtelli, as he brought Cynthia into the station. "See if she wants something to drink. The sheriff will be with her in a few minutes."

Half an hour later, Sheriff Berkson walked into Room Two. He smiled at Cynthia and sat down. "You comfortable, Cynthia?" he asked.

"You know what, Sheriff? I've had a rough day. Just ask what you want to ask, and let me get the hell out of here."

"Where were you last Saturday night?"

"I think you know. I was with Bobby – all night."

"Were you out drinking with him earlier in the evening?"

"I told you. All night."

"Before you met Bobby at Waxy's, did you have dinner at Doctor White's house?"

Cynthia looked like a deer caught in headlights. Her face froze, her eyes glazed over, and she stopped breathing for a second or two. Then, she smiled. "You got me."

"So, you did have dinner with him. Who else was there?"

"Just a couple of other people. Nobody important," she replied.

"Oh, I think they're very important," the sheriff said. "Who else was there, Cynthia?"

"Well, you don't have to get mad at me. There were just a couple of us. The doctor, Sylvia, and me. I left early, though."

"Was Michael McMillan there?"

"Maybe."

"Maybe? What do you mean, maybe?"

"I need to talk to my lawyer."

"You don't need a lawyer. Answer the question."

"I don't like the way you're talking to me, Sheriff. I'm done answering your questions," Cynthia said.

"You're done when I say you're done. Was McMillan there or not?"

"I'm supposed to say he was there," she said, starting to cry."

"Why are you supposed to say that?" the sheriff asked.

"Doctor White said I should say he was there if you asked me. He called me a little while ago and told me to say that."

"So, McMillan wasn't there?"

"No. It was just the three of us. Wally told her he was having a party, but that was just to get her there."

"For what reason?"

"We wanted her to tell the truth about Melissa's murder. I wanted her to tell me that Bobby did it, so Big John could get out of prison."

Sheriff Berkson sat back in his chair and looked at her. She was sobbing now, the tears running down her face. He handed her a box of Kleenex.

"So, you and White killed her?"

"God, no. She was more than alive when I left. It just got out of hand. Wally got physical with her. The more she refused to admit that Bobby and she had framed Big John, the madder he got. He couldn't let her go. She would have gone to the police. You, probably. He had to get rid of her."

"Let me get this straight, Cynthia. Dr. White and you invited her, under false pretenses, to his house so you could try to get her to admit Bobby killed his mother. Is that correct?"

"Yes, but she wasn't supposed to die. I'm so sorry. I just love Big John so much. I wanted him to come home."

"I can understand that part of your story. What I don't understand is what White was getting out of it. What difference did it make to him if Bobby killed his mother or not?

"I told him if he got Sylvia to say Bobby did it, I would sleep with him."

"You weren't having an affair with him? What about those pictures he took?"

"I just let him take those pictures so he would help me. It never went any further than that." Sylvia stared into space for a few seconds, then, said, "I guess I do owe him, though. Do you think I still need to sleep with him, Sheriff?"

"I think you've done enough, Cynthia," he replied.

"Can I go home now?"

"Sorry, Cynthia. You're under arrest. I'm afraid I'm gonna have to hold you here until Monday."

"What for?" I didn't do anything wrong. I don't want to stay here."

"You conspired against Sylvia Toppers and she died because of your actions. You're an accessory to murder."

"I am not. I didn't hurt her. It was Wally. Please," she sobbed, "let me go home."

"I can't do that. I can call Judge Peterson and see if he'll have a bond hearing for you tomorrow. If he sets bail, you will probably be able to go home tomorrow."

"Then, I won't be arrested anymore?"

"No, Cynthia. That's not the way it works. If the judge lets you out on bond, you have to promise to stay around and show up for your trial."

"There's going to be a trial?" she cried, sobbing even louder.

Sheriff Berkson opened the door and yelled, "Funtelli, get in here."

Officer Funtelli walked over to interrogation Room Two and stuck his head in the door. "You want me, Sheriff?"

"Please show Ms. Hughes to a cell. Make sure it's a clean one. Get her some blankets and a pillow."

"She's spending the night, Sheriff?"

"Yeah, she's spending the night."

Sheriff Berkson left Cynthia with Funtelli and opened the door to interrogation Room One. McMillan looked up, as he entered the room. "Now, what the hell do you want?"

"You are free to leave. Officer Herzberg will give you a ride home. I'm sorry for any inconvenience we've caused you," the sheriff said.

"That's it? You're sorry? Damn right you're sorry. You're a sorry piece of shit, that's what you are."

"Mr. McMillan. I apologize. Please excuse me." the sheriff said and left the room.

"You going home, Casey, or do you want to ride over to the hospital with me?"

"You got that bastard?"

"We've got him," the sheriff replied, a big grin spreading over his face. "Cynthia poured her little heart out."

Saturday Morning

On Saturday morning, Judge Peterson called a special session of court for a bail hearing. A court-appointed lawyer pled her case, and the judge set her bond at $100,000.00.

"I don't have that kind of money," she told the judge. He explained to her that she only needed ten percent of that amount, and she started to cry.

"It doesn't make any difference," she said. "I don't have $20,000.00."

"Ten thousand," said the judge. "Do you know someone who can post it for you?"

"Maybe my aunt will. I could call her. Do you have a phone I can use?"

"Sheriff, will you bring Ms. Hughes back to my chambers, so she can use my phone?"

Sheriff Berkson looked at Judge Peterson, wondering what had gotten into him. Unless there was a trial in progress, the judge never allowed anyone in his chambers. He glanced over at Cynthia, who was still sobbing, and noticed that the first four buttons of her blouse were undone. Mystery solved.

"My aunt's not home," Cynthia told the judge. "Can I make another call?"

"Of course, my dear," the judge told her. "You call as many people as you need to get that bail money."

"Maybe, you could just lower the amount," she said. "That might help."

"I can't do that. It's on record now. How about your parents? Could they help you?"

"I don't think so," Cynthia said. "Wait, I know someone who might help me."

She dialed a number and waited, holding her breath. Then, she smiled and said, "Hi, Bobby."

A few hours later Cynthia and Bobby were standing in front of the courthouse.

"Aren't you going to give me a ride?" Cynthia asked him.

"I don't think so. I'm going in the other direction."

"Well, how am I supposed to get home?"

"Not my problem, babe," Bobby answered her and walked over to his car.

"Bobby, please," she yelled.

He stopped and looked at her, disgust showing on his face. "Getting you out of jail is the last thing I'm ever going to do for you. I only did that because that's what my brother would have wanted me to do. But, you're on your own from now on, Cynthia. Don't call me again."

"I'm sorry, Bobby. Please, don't hate me."

"You got Sylvia killed. She was a good person and she never hurt anybody. You are responsible for her death. Maybe that White guy pulled the trigger, but it's your fucking fault. I shouldn't hate you? I hate your fucking guts. Just stay away from me."

Cynthia stood there, tears running down her cheeks, and watched him drive away.

Bobby Johnson

The church service had been attended by about one hundred people. Most of those people were now standing by Sylvia's grave, listening to the minister say the final prayer. After everyone left the cemetery, her casket would be lowered into the ground.

Bobby had flown down to Texas the night before. He planned to fly back to Hollister in a few hours.

The thought that he would never see Sylvia again, brought Bobby to tears. He had truly loved her and she was lost to him forever. Damn that Cynthia, he thought. Her obsession that he had murdered his mother had caused this, he thought. Why couldn't she just have left well enough alone?

As he walked to his rental car, Olivia approached him, smiling a sad smile.

"Are you coming back to the house for refreshments, Bobby?" she asked.

"I thought I'd stop by for a while before I head back," he replied.

"I'll be up in a couple of weeks," Olivia said. "I've got to get her house ready for market and I guess I'll have an estate sale."

"I can help you with that if you want," Bobby said.

"Really? That's so nice of you. I'll probably need some help."

"Why don't you call me when you plan on coming up? I'll send the plane for you."

"Seriously? You'd do that for me? That's so nice of you. But I'd thought I'd drive up, so I can take some of her things back with me."

"Take the plane, Olivia. We'll put those things on the plane with you to take home. It should make it easier for you, especially if you're traveling alone."

"I might just do that, Bobby. My ex is taking care of the girls. You are so sweet. Thank you."

"Just give me a call when you're ready," Bobby said.

"I'll do that. It's easy to see why Sylvia loved you, Bobby."

On the flight home, Bobby's mind wouldn't stop thinking about what Olivia had said. Sylvia had told her sister that she loved him. He wondered how two people could love each other and not share that knowledge. He had never told her and she had never told him.

We shared so much, he thought, and yet we were both afraid to take our relationship to the next level and commit. Now it was too late. Damn Cynthia and that doctor. Damn them to hell.

He pushed the call button. Annie, his attendant who was sitting in a seat just across from him, looked up from her book.

"I'm right here, Bobby," she said.

Bobby smiled. "Sorry, I guess I'm someplace else. How about making me a nice strong drink? I'm tired and that's probably the only way I'm gonna fall asleep."

"I've got an Ambien, if you want one," she said.

"No thanks. Just the drink, please."

"You want to talk?" Annie asked him.

"I just want to sleep."

"I'm sorry about your friend, Bobby. I'll get you that drink."

Three hours later, Bobby was back on the ground and driving home. He punched a speed dial number on his phone and waited for an answer.

"Hello,"

"You want the house back? Meet me there tomorrow at ten," he said and hung up.

He pulled into his driveway, parked the car, and let himself into his home. He slipped out of his shoes, and without bothering to get undressed, laid down on his bed and immediately fell asleep.

At nine the next morning, Bobby placed a call to the Hollister Police Department and left a message, asking that Sheriff Berkson call him as soon as arrived at work. Brad called the sheriff, who was having breakfast at Minnie's Diner, and relayed the message.

"Did he say what it was about?" the sheriff asked him.

"Just that he wanted to talk to you."

"You got his number handy? I'll call him now."

Sheriff Berkson wrote the number on a paper napkin and hung up.

"What's up?" Casey asked.

"Bobby Johnson called."

"What's he want?"

"I'm about to find out," the sheriff said, as he called Bobby.

"Hello," Bobby answered.

"Morning, Bobby. Sheriff Berkson here. You called?"

"Sheriff, I just wanted to inform you that I'm meeting Cynthia at noon. We're gonna discuss what items she wants to take out of the house. Is it at all possible that one of your officers could be present?"

"I'm glad to see you're being careful around her, Bobby. I think I can arrange somebody for you. It'll probably be Officer Funtelli. He seems to be the only one that doesn't trip over his tongue when he's around her."

Bobby laughed. "I know what you mean. Thanks a lot, Sheriff. I owe you one."

"Anything to keep the peace," the sheriff said.

The Final Chapter

Cynthia looked at herself in the mirror and smiled. I look sooo good, she thought and wondered how any man could resist her. She was happy. Bobby was giving her the house back and everything would be back to normal soon. She wasn't concerned about the upcoming trial. All she needed was for her attorney to make sure the majority of jurors we men. There was no doubt, in her mind, that they would find her not guilty.

Cynthia looked at her watch. It was 9:30 and she decided it was time to leave. She had time to spare, but she wanted to be sure she didn't keep Bobby waiting. She didn't want to give him a reason to get upset and change his mind.

Bobby drove up to the house and parked behind the squad car. Cynthia's car was parked in the driveway. He glanced at his watch. It was 12:10.

He got out and walked over to the squad car and knocked on the window. Officer Funtelli jumped, the noise waking him. He looked over at Bobby, smiled, and exited the car.

"Sorry I scared you," Bobby said.

Funtelli laughed. "Don't tell the sheriff I was sleeping on the job. He'll never let me forget it."

"He won't hear it from me. Is Cynthia in her car?"

"I think she's inside already," Funtelli replied.

"Really? I guess she must have had another key. Well, let's get this over with."

"So, just what's happening today? The sheriff only told me to be here by noon and make sure you two didn't come to blows."

"I told Cynthia she could pick up the rest of her stuff. I don't know what furniture is hers, but I figure Big John bought most of what is here. If there's something she wants, I'll probably give it to her."

Officer Funtelli and Bobby walked up the steps to the front door. Bobby started to open the door but realized the door was still locked.

"It's locked," he said to Funtelli. "Let me get the key."

Funtelli watched as Bobby reached into his pocket and pulled out a key ring. He found the one he was looking for, inserted it into the keyhole, and opened the door.

"Cynthia?" he called out, as he and Funtelli walked into an empty room.

There was no response.

"She might be upstairs," Bobby commented. He walked to the stairs and yelled, "Cynthia, are you up there?"

Again, there was no response.

"Well, her car's here. She's got to be here someplace."

"Maybe, she's in the backyard," Funtelli said.

"Why don't you check there and I'll look upstairs," Bobby suggested.

"Will do," replied Funtelli, and headed towards the kitchen. As he started towards the back door, he noticed that the door to the basement was open and the light leading down the stairs was on.

He walked over and glanced down the stairs. He took a few steps and then hesitated. After taking a deep breath, he went the rest of the way into the basement.

"Damn, what a waste," he mumbled to himself. After deciding there was nothing he could do, he went back up the stairs to the kitchen and took out his phone.

"Brad, give me the sheriff."

"Why are you calling the sheriff?" Bobby asked as he walked into the kitchen.

Funtelli waved at him to be quiet. "Sheriff, I'm over at Big John's house. Cynthia's dead. It looks like she hung herself."

Bobby looked at him in shock. He started towards the basement door, but Funtelli grabbed his arm. "You can't go down there, Bobby," he said.

"But I've got to help her," Bobby exclaimed.

"Bobby, listen to me. There's nothing you can do. Sit down."

"What's going on, Funtelli?" the sheriff yelled.

"I'm trying to calm Bobby down. Sheriff, can you get Doc Harris over here?"

"Don't touch anything," Sheriff Berkson ordered.

Officer Funtelli looked over at the counter. "Wait, I think I just found a note," he told the sheriff.

"You got gloves?"

"I do. Hold on a minute," Funtelli replied.

He gloved up and carefully opened the note. "Sheriff, it's from Cynthia."

"What does it say," Sheriff Berkson asked.

"It's hard to read, like she was really shaking when she wrote it," said Funtelli.

"Just read it to me," the sheriff yelled.

"It says, 'Tell my parents I'm sorry. I don't want to go on living without my Big John."

"Damn," said Sheriff Berkson. "I never would have expected that from her."

"Life is sure full of surprises, isn't it, Sheriff?"

Bobby Johnson was by his pool, soaking up the sun. The weather was starting to get cool, and it wouldn't be long before winter would show its ugly side. They didn't get much snow in Hollister. It was usually just cold enough to freeze, and the residents and Branson's winter vacationers would deal with icy roads instead of freshly plowed streets. Bobby didn't really care. If the weather got nasty, he would leave for a few weeks and fly off to some warm, sunny location. It made no difference where he was. He would still spend his hour or so a day swimming in his heated pool or at some fancy resort.

It was one day shy of two weeks since Officer Funtelli had found Cynthia hanging in the basement. The coroner, Doc Harris, had determined that her death was a suicide. Not many people showed up for her funeral. Bobby went and paid his condolences to the family. He couldn't tell her parents enough times how sorry he was for their loss. Big John had asked to be allowed out of prison to attend, but the warden denied his request.

Bobby was still hurting, feeling his loss of Sylvia. It's strange, he thought, that sometimes you don't know how much a person means to you until you lose them. He thought his mother meant a lot to him, but he hardly missed her after he killed her. I guess there is something wrong with me, he thought. I've killed two people now and I don't have one regret.

He smiled a little smile, as he thought of Sylvia's sister, Olivia. They looked so much alike that it was almost scary. She would be coming up soon to take care of Sylvia's estate. He could hardly wait.

About the Author

I was born in Idaho in 1939. My father's job demanded that we frequently move so, by the age of ten, I had lived in Idaho, Montana, Colorado, Michigan, and, finally Wisconsin. I lived in Wisconsin for the next eight years, until I graduated from school.

I am the proud mother of three wonderful sons and two fantastic grandsons.

I worked as an accountant for most of my life. Two years before I retired, I did a complete switch in careers and managed two Curves fitness facilities in Illinois. I retired in 2002 and moved to Branson, MO. In 2012, I moved to Indiana to be closer to my family and have lived in Highland for the past three and a half years.

I enjoy a good laugh and figure it's my sense of humor that has kept me going when times were tough. Reading has always been one of my passions and I still read a couple of books a week.

In 2003 I started designing websites for a few clubs and I maintain them in my spare time. I also designed my own site, so please feel free to visit.

For most of my life, I have written short stories and poems for amusement. I wrote *Blueberries and Bears and My Brother's Shoes*, a story about growing up in the forties and fifties. After I self-published it and gave it to friends and family to read, they encouraged me to get serious about my writing.

Crossing Sydney was my first novel and it was published in July 2015. It has received outstanding reviews. A sequence to this book is being considered at this time.

Don't Smother Your Mother was my second book, and I had fun writing it. Although it's a mystery, I threw humor into it and made it an easy-to-read whodunit. *A Bad Week in Hollister* picks up where this one leaves off, with another mystery for Sheriff "Cowboy" Berkson to solve.

I never thought that, at the age of 76, I would become an author. I certainly am enjoying my retirement knowing, that when I get up each morning, I have something to look forward to.

Visit me at: www.susanlpare.com.

www.ingramcontent.com/pod-product-compliance
Lightning Source LLC
Chambersburg PA
CBHW070625130626
46556CB00001B/472